FORLORN HOPE

A DONNER PARTY STORY

Best regards, to
you and Joanne, Jinicus

[signature]

ALSO BY JACK RICHARDS

Dormant Enhancement I

Dormant Enhancement II

Return – Four Novellas

FORLORN HOPE

A DONNER PARTY STORY

BY

JACK RICHARDS

Bookstand Publishing

www.bookstandpublishing.com

Published by
Bookstand Publishing
Morgan Hill, CA 95037
4177_3

ISBN 978-1-61863-932-5

Printed in the United States of America

For my family

Linda, Laurie, Karen, and Grant

"never take no cutoffs and hury along as fast as you can."

… Letter from Virginia Reed

PROLOGUE

*I*nside a dark cabin the faint glow of burning coals provides enough light to see the man as he moves out of the darkness toward the embers. He thrusts a stick into the coals and waits for several seconds before he withdraws it. The burning end illuminates the room.

An old woman lies in a bed. Her mouth slowly opens and her head rolls weakly from side to side. The man, dirty, unkempt, and with a full beard, grasps the grimy blanket and throws it back to reveal the frail and grizzled body. He grabs the ankle of the emaciated woman and pulls the body from the bed. Her head makes a dull thud as it hits the dirt floor. He drags the body toward a flap of canvas that serves as the door. When he pulls the canvas flap aside, the fading light of dusk further illuminates the hovel. Outside, the snow reaches past the top of the cabin.

The look on the man's face reflects the ardor of his intentions as he drags the body across the surface of the snow. He travels only a short distance before turning and dropping to his knees in front of the body. He pulls a large knife from its sheath and begins his gruesome task.

Minutes later, a growing circle of red surrounds the nearly naked body, gutted and missing a leg.

The man, now covered with blood, rises and moves away. In one hand he carries the liver and entrails; the other grasps the severed leg by the ankle, trailing it in the snow behind him as he stumbles away.

1

TEN MONTHS EARLIER – BELLEVILLE, ILLINOIS, APRIL 10, 1846

To provide his wife with those few precious moments of sleep before she is jolted awake by the sounds of their two children, William has taken to silently easing out of bed and peeking into the children's room even before the first hint of morning light. Secure in the knowledge that they are all right, he gently pushes their door closed until it is only open a crack. Margaret, barely a year old, is usually the first to stir, but fortunately seems to be content to entertain herself with gentle cooing sounds as she studies the interior of her crib or plays with the doll her mother places next to her. James, at three years of age, is oblivious to these sounds and often remains asleep until awakened.

William Eddy's workday begins before the first rays of the sun are visible in the East. After routinely splashing cold water on his face and vigorously drying it on a towel, he dresses, walks from their small three-room house to his workshop, located no more than twenty feet away, lights the kerosene lamp, and builds the fire he uses to forge the metal used in the building of his carriages.

Born in South Carolina, William was the oldest of eleven children. As a result, he was forced to be both responsible and industrious at an early age. It also may have accounted for his desire to escape his family duties and seek his fortune, independent of others, in the Great American West. Therefore, as soon as the opportunity presented itself, he left his family, with the objective of becoming a frontiersman. He became a skilled hunter, but soon realized that something more substantial might be required for him to truly benefit from the opportunities this great country offered. His interest in working with his hands resulted in an apprenticeship to a carriage maker. More than an apt pupil, he soon became highly proficient and eager to establish his own shop. As fate would have it, while passing through Belleville he met a delightful young lady at a church social. Her long, dark hair was pulled back from her face and allowed to fall freely. At first he did not fully appreciate the beauty of her perfectly formed features, perhaps because her dark eyes were downcast and seemingly reflective of a melancholy nature. Upon further scrutiny, however, he saw in her a kindness and a charm that immediately captured his heart. Love quickly blossomed for both, and soon they were married. With the help of Eleanor's father, the newly married couple established residence, and William opened his shop while Eleanor continued in her post as a schoolteacher. William's work as a carriage maker quickly earned him the respect of many. After their first child Eleanor chose to remain at home to care for what they hoped would be a large family.

Though William and Eleanor became successful and respected members of the community, William's desire to become a part of the westward expansion still burned brightly. But, for now, his focus had to remain on the present. Eleanor happily cared for their home and their children, and William spent his workday filling the requests from his growing list of customers.

On this beautiful spring morning, William is so busily engaged in putting the finishing touches on an open carriage that he does not notice a man enter his shop. Though wearing an informal but fashionable frock coat, the visitor is clearly a member of the upper class. The manner in which he enters the shop and looks around conveys a certain attitude and station in life that sets him apart from the laboring class. He watches William perform his craft for several seconds before he announces his presence.

"Excuse me, Mr. Eddy?"

William, now aware that he is not alone, looks up and wipes his hands on a rag before he rises to greet what he must assume is a potential customer.

"Yes, sir. What can I do for you?"

2

"Name's Reed. I need some work done on a spare wheel for one of my wagons. Can you do it?"

"Wagons?"

"I have three. Two for my goods and one for my family."

"What kind 'a wagons?"

"Take a look."

Outside, the two men approach a wagon and its team of oxen next to the dirt road that passes near the front of Eddy's small frame house. Eddy stops short to get a good look at it.

"Mr. Reed, that's quite a handsome design. Looks like you've had some special alterations done."

"It's my design. If you'll notice, we have doors on the side with steps to climb aboard. Look inside if you like. You'll see that I've made every effort to provide the proper accommodations for my family on our trip."

"Trip? May I ask how far you intend to travel?"

"Can't say exactly how far. Maybe 2500 miles. We're headed to California."

"California!"

"That's right. The 'Promised Land' for those of a hardy mind and spirit."

"I envy you, Sir. It's something I've dreamed about for some time."

Reed smiles and replies: "Why dream? Make it real. A man in your trade and with your knowledge could be a valuable asset to all of us."

"All of us?"

"We set out from Springfield four days ago with three families in nine wagons. Including our employees there were thirty-two of us. It's our plan to join up with others along the way and finally become a part of the Great Overland Caravan. Perhaps you've heard talk of it. Their plan

3

is to leave Independence in early May and drive to Fort Hall. From there they will take the Fremont Route to the bay of San Francisco. You'd be a welcome addition to our party. We'll be here another night adding to our stock, so you have time to get organized if you're a mind to."

With visions of a new life for himself and his family dancing in his head, Eddy remains silent. Finally, Mr. Reed breaks the silence with, "The wheel, Mr. Eddy?"

"Oh, yes, Sir. Let's have a look."

Fascinated, Eleanor's two children watch their mother carefully fold and mold the cookie dough before she flattens it and sprinkles a spoonful of flour on its surface. Her every move is accompanied by the tune she hums that highlights the actions of her delicate hands.

Preceded by a gentle kiss to James' cheek, she places the cookie cutter in his hand and directs it to a position on the surface of the dough. Delighted with the responsibility of forming the cookie, he smiles and presses it. The shape of a dog appears after he lifts it, requiring an immediate desire to form another. After he does so, Eleanor suggests that the big brother show his baby sister how the difficult task is accomplished, giving him the responsibility and opportunity to be a teacher.

James smiles, takes the cutter, and places it in his sister's hand, all the while using his version of baby talk that is designed to communicate the complex technique. To be expected, the cutter goes directly into the baby's mouth. Perplexed, James tries to re-direct it to the dough's surface. His mother's laugh, followed by her words, "Maybe we should bake them first, sweetheart," relieves him of his responsibility, so he joins her in their little joke with a superior laugh of his own.

Eleanor produces another cutter, this one in the shape of a cat, and gives it to James, leaving Margaret free to enjoy her new toy. James quickly returns to a focus on his original duty. As he does so, the kitchen door opens and William, with a big smile on his face, enters. Clearly excited, he bends down to give both children a kiss before he turns to his wife. "And how are you, Mrs. Eddy?"

4

Somewhat confused, but pleased by his appearance at this time of day, she carefully extracts the cutter from Margaret and replaces it with a toy before she picks her up and sets her down in her crib. Though she follows this with a re-shaping of the cookie dough for an eager James, she devotes her full attention to her husband. "Things are fine here. Your day must be going well."

"Oh, Ellie, you can't imagine what an opportunity has come our way." He takes her hand and leads her to a chair. "The wagon I worked on today belongs to a Mr. James Reed from Springfield. I wish you'd seen it. It's just for his family. He has two other wagons to carry their supplies. The family wagon has every comfort you could imagine. You enter through a specially built door on the side. It's the closest thing to a fancy hotel room I've seen. Inside, it has two levels. On the lower level the seats are set on springs to make the ride a smooth one. There are bunks on the upper level and, believe this or not, a little stove with the stovepipe running up and out the top."

"My lord! A real stove?"

"A *real* stove. What's more, there's a small library… a spinning wheel … a place to make a meal, imagine that! There was a stuffed chair, and, oh yes, a mirror, a big mirror next to a chest of drawers, and hangers for their clothes."

"Sounds … marvelous. Where are they going?"

"California."

"California? How nice. But you said something about an opportunity that's come our way. What did you mean?"

"He invited us to join their train."

"Join them? To California?"

"Yes. It's our chance at a new life, Ellie."

Unable to grasp the full significance of her husband's statement, she remains silent. This gives William the opportunity to continue his argument. "They're here overnight and are spendin' tomorrow organizin' and restockin'. It gives us enough time to get ready."

"Ready to do what?"

"Join them."

"But how? *Why* would we?"

"It's *California*, sweetheart. The whole country's lookin' West. There's land for the takin'. And riches. A new home – a new life. Don't you see, Ellie, we can't let this pass us by."

Finding her voice, she continues a counter-argument. "This is our home – here. Our family ... our friends ... your business. It's all right here. Why would we risk losing everything?"

"That's just it. We'd not be *losin'* – we'd be grabbin' the opportunity to create something. It's the right time for us – for our family to be a part of somethin' exciting. It's the place for us to grow – to be a part of this country's future."

"But ... how could we –"

"Our wagon's more than adequate to make the trip. It's not as fancy as Mr. Reed's, but it's certainly solid. We'd not travel in luxury, maybe, but we're not accustomed to livin' that way anyway."

"Who are these people? Why would they ... how would we fit?"

"I met some of the folks today. Mr. Reed, as I told you, is wealthy. He had a successful business in Springfield and didn't hesitate a moment to leave it behind for somethin' even better. His wife and their three children are with him, and there's a daughter from an earlier marriage. His wife's mother is also travelin' with them. Back in Springfield they combined with brothers - George and Jacob Donner and their families. Both of the Donners are in their fifties and were well established and prosperous farmers. Their families on the trip number better 'n sixteen. So you see, there was no hesitation on their part to look for a new life. Their plan is to join an Oregon caravan in Independence and travel with them to Ft. Hood, Idaho. That's where they'll break off and take a route that leads to the Bay of San Francisco."

"That's all wonderful for them, but ..."

"But what, Ellie? They see the promise of a bright future for their families. Why can't we?"

"Because we're not ... frontier folk. We can't –"

"Neither are they, don't you see?"

"But they're established. They're folks of substance."

"Listen to what you're sayin', Ellie. What does 'folks of substance' have to do with it? There's no reluctance on their part to leave what they had for the promise of somethin' better. What gamble would we be takin'? We're young and full of energy and we'd be givin' our kids the chance of a future filled with unbelievable opportunities. And, *it's California*! Limitless prime farmland just for the takin'. A healthy climate for the children, free from these damnable freezin' winters and miserable hot summers – a land of perpetual springtime."

"Why does it have to be *now* – all of a sudden?"

"If not now, when?"

"When the kids are older. When we can make proper plans. When we've had time to talk to our families. When –"

"There'll always be another 'when.' Everythin' we've always wanted can happen now."

"What is it we don't have *now*?"

"Land, for one thing. Opportunity for us and for our kids to be part of a new world – to do and *be* anything we want."

"It sounds like … you've decided then."

"I know how you feel, darlin'. I promise you I'll take care of you and the kids. You'll have nothin' to worry about."

Eleanor speaks softly, as to herself. "Everything I want is here … now."

"We just can't let this pass us by, Ellie."

"When would we have to leave?"

"That's just it. Tomorrow."

"Tomorrow! That's impossible, William."

"No it's not. We'll just have to get busy." Bubbling over with enthusiasm, he ignores her despondency as he moves toward the door. "I

7

have things to do. Let me take care of them, and then we can begin to pack. Ah, Ellie, it'll be great. You'll see!" With that, he vanishes, leaving Eleanor staring into a void.

Numbed by the shock of having her world turned upside down, Eleanor remains seated as the voices in her head begin to demand answers:

"Did he say tomorrow?"

"Leave? Our home? William's business? Our life?"

"What will my parents say?"

"Why California? What do I care about California?"

"How can the kids make such a trip?"

"What can I say ... must I say to change his mind?"

With no answers forthcoming, she seeks a release from her fears and finds it in her children's impatience with her inattention to their needs. Her escape succeeds as she begins to reshape the dough for James to continue his assignment while, at the same time, she speaks to the baby in the soothing voice of a loving mother.

Buoyed by the impression that he had received his wife's consent to make the move, William begins a frenzy of activity. Deciding to first confront the most difficult task of all, he walks directly to the home of Eleanor's parents to inform them of their plan. It would, of course, be a shock for them to hear that their daughter and their grandchildren were leaving, but he would also be giving them notice that the home and carriage shop, both of which they were renting from her parents, would be vacated.

Expecting the worst, William is not surprised at the almost hysterical reaction from Eleanor's mother who almost collapses and begins to sob uncontrollably before she can be helped into a chair. Perhaps to provide a much-needed stability for his wife, whose world is crumbling about her, her husband maintains a stoic demeanor and says very little. His body language, however, indicates to his son-in-law that he not only understands, but actually admires their decision to make a

8

new life for themselves – this, of course, communicated subtly and out of sight from his wife.

With this unpleasant duty out of the way, William's spirit soars. He returns home to get their horde of cash from under their mattress to begin the purchase of the many essentials needed for the trip. He is surprised to find Eleanor in the same place he'd left her, playing with the children as though nothing had happened. The moment he tells her what he's done, however, she breaks into tears and immediately leaves the room.

Undeterred by his wife's reaction and convinced that it is the result of her having to leave her parents, he speaks to his wife behind the closed door. "You'd best be getting the things together you want to take with us. I'll be back as soon as I buy what we need." He waits for an answer, but when there is none he decides to postpone any further discussion and leave. Before he leaves he gives both children a kiss and then speaks to James. "Tell your mother I'll be back as soon as I can."

After informing Mr. Reed of their intention to join their party, he spends time introducing himself to the members of their company and getting their advice on dozens of seemingly small but enormously important lessons of life in a wagon moving westward, and with the help of his father-in-law hurriedly begins to acquire the necessities. Numbered among the many required things are a team of oxen, two beef cattle, a cow to provide milk for the children, and a saddle horse. And, of course, a trusty rifle and two pistols with a good supply of powder and an adequate amount of lead to make bullets.

William returns home twice to check on his wife's progress and to inform her of the suggestions made by several women in the party, most notably those offered by Tamsen and Elizabeth Donner, the wives of the Donner brothers from Springfield. Though non-committal and detached, Eleanor is busy gathering what she considers to be the "treasures" she cannot do without. His effort to communicate with his wife is met by a blank look that mirrors her forced acceptance of her husband's decision. He decides to take it upon himself to purchase or trade for the recommended items: a stock of flour, salt, sugar, coffee, bacon and other selected meats. Without comment or direction from him, he assumes that the domestic niceties (such things as utensils, soap, dishes, clothing, and small items of furniture) would be left to Eleanor's discretion.

After coming to grips with the inevitable, Eleanor's mother joins her daughter late in the afternoon and does her best to put on a brave front. They both make an effort to avoid an expression of their sorrow and impending heartache by concentrating on the task of selecting and packing for the trip. When William returns he immediately feels like an intruder in this oppressive setting, so he remains for only a few minutes before he excuses himself to resume his myriad of activities.

It is shortly before midnight when William's flurry of activity ceases. When he enters the house he finds the two ladies quietly sitting in front of a stack of boxes having a cup of tea. They barely look up when he enters, though Eleanor, almost as though sleepwalking, rises and pours him a cup of tea without comment. Unsure just what to say, and wisely choosing not to express his growing excitement and anxiety, William joins them in a quiet contemplation of what their lives would be like from this moment on.

In bed, long after he and his wife have eased under the sheets without a word, he lies awake staring at the ceiling, playing out in his mind the many frustrations he had encountered while trying to complete his numerous obligations. Grudgingly, and fighting the urge to get up and continue the effort to make ready their ability to leave in the morning, he finally accepts the fact that their departure might have to be delayed a day, or possibly two.

Why am I so conflicted? The opportunity of a lifetime presents itself, and I should rejoice. But the unhappiness it is causing my wife and her family cannot be ignored. Is it wise to abandon my successful business and to lose my acceptance by a growing community? Will life in a new environment be everything I've heard? Will there be dangers on the trip? Am I capable of keeping my promise to my wife that, "I would take care of her and the kids, and she would have nothing to worry about."? But it's

California! - everyone's dream! Adventure. Excitement.
Unlimited opportunities. The possibility of riches - of
becoming comfortably established...

A mysterious force jolts him awake, and he sits bolt upright even before the first light of dawn. He looks at the clock: 4:00 A.M. Aware that his movements might have woken up his wife, he slowly eases back and rests his head on the pillow to review his earlier thoughts and to plan a way to get out of bed without robbing his wife of her necessary sleep. Several minutes later he quietly slides one leg out from under the covers and reaches for the floor. Before he can plant his foot, Ellie's voice breaks the silence: "Don't wake the kids."

"Sorry. I tried to be quiet. How long have you been awake?"

"I never went to sleep."

"Oh ... I wish we'd ... Ellie, I know how you feel about this, but won't you try to see this as I do?"

"I've tried, but all I can think of is what we're giving up for ... for something that scares me to death."

"What's there to be afraid of?"

"Of not knowing what's out there. Of giving up the happiness of our life here and now."

"Well, it's our chance, and I'm not going to let us miss it!" Even as he is saying this he regrets the tone of his voice – of the manner in which he feels compelled to assert his position as head of the family. He knows he's wrong to deny the wife he loves so dearly the thing that is at the core of her happiness for his own selfish ambitions.

Selfish? Is it really selfish? It is, after all, for the good of
the whole family. She'll soon see I was right. She might be
unhappy for the moment, perhaps, but she'll soon be
eternally grateful to me for the beautiful life that lies
ahead.

While hurriedly dressing, eager both to remove himself from this unpleasant scene and to notify Mr. Reed as soon as possible of his decision to delay their departure, he is halted by Eleanor's voice, subservient, but insistent. "William, have you really given the proper amount of thought to this decision?"

Unsure as to what the most effective, yet sensitive approach should be to accomplish his goal, he stammers something like, "Yes, I have. I know how you ..." Then, in a very decisive tone, "Listen, Ellie, we *are going*, not today maybe, but as soon as I can take care of all the necessary details ... so please do what you have to, but be packed and ready to leave as soon as possible." To add force to his uncompromising edict, he turns and walks out of the room without another word.

Eleanor slowly sits on the bed and lowers her head. She remains this way for several seconds before she hears the sounds of her kids coming toward her room. She stands, wipes her eyes, and creates a bright and welcoming smile.

The "necessary details" William spoke of included communicating to his apprentice the information and description of the numerous jobs he had underway or which were promised to his customers, settling several accounts with his creditors, loading the wagon, and disposing of a rather large number of possessions that could not be taken on the trip. As he methodically works his way through his list, new matters arise that have to be taken care of before he can leave. The first thing he does upon exiting the house is to convey to Mr. Reed the information of his delayed departure. He is greatly relieved to hear Mr. Reed's assurance that a two or even three-day delay would not spoil William's plans. He even gives him a detailed map of the route the train will follow along with the assurance that a single wagon could easily close the ground and catch them within a few days.

"Mr. Eddy, our goal is to reach Independence by the first of May. You have adequate time to reach us before then, but if not I would strongly advise you to not travel alone beyond that point because that is where we enter Indian territory. Our large number virtually guarantees our safety from then on. Our group plans to leave this morning, but the trail will be easy for you to follow. May I say that I am delighted that you will be joining us. A man of your talents will be a valuable asset. I wish you the best of luck and a safe journey."

2

ON THE TRAIL

The original party consisting of the three families that formed in Springfield left Belleville on the morning of the eleventh. After watching the wagons depart, William sets about to complete his tasks as quickly as possible. He also does his best to assuage his feeling of guilt over his abrupt and insensitive manner with Eleanor by displaying as much affection as possible toward her and the children each time he returns home during the day. His every effort, however, is met by his wife's blank and emotionless, but dutiful, responses. Though she is actively engaged in making ready for the move, it is obviously being done without a hint of enthusiasm. It continues this way for two days, and by the end of the second day, William declares things "ready to go."

So, by mid-morning on the fourteenth of April the Eddy family say their goodbyes to Eleanor's parents and to a rather large number of friends who have gathered to wish them well. Their lone wagon, with their limited number of livestock trailing behind, pulls away from the front of their house. While Eleanor fights back her tears for the sake of her confused children, William stares straight ahead as though looking for the open door to a life of adventure and riches galore.

Reed's estimate of approximately ten to twelve miles a day to cover the nearly 250 miles between Belleville and Independence would put them there to meet up with the larger party near the first of May. Though warned to not drive his oxen too much beyond that, William feels that by leaving early in the morning and limiting their number of breaks during the day to two, they would catch up to the slower traveling wagon train before they reached Independence with plenty of time to spare.

Though William is accustomed to spending time in the wilderness, it is a new experience for the rest of his family. Trackless valleys of waving grass, glimpses of all forms of wildlife, rapidly flowing streams, and magnificently beautiful wildflowers thrill them all. Even Eleanor's misgivings about their decision to leave begin to disappear as she surveys her surroundings – that is until she sees the two Indians standing near the trail. Though William hardly takes notice of their presence, Eleanor grows tense as she puts an arm around each of her two children.

The two Indians, though never taking their eyes off them, stand completely motionless as the wagon passes. Moments later, as they grow ever smaller in Eleanor's eyes, they remain unmoved.

"Are they..."

"What?" answers William, "Dangerous?"

"Yes."

"Not likely. Just curious, same as you. I'm not saying they couldn't cause some trouble, but in this part of the country it's more dangerous for them to act up than it would be in the Indian Territory. That's why we need to catch up with the others. There's definitely safety in numbers."

"But ... we're *alone!*"

"Not really. There are several trading posts along the way. These Indians must be pretty civilized if they're here. Besides, I was ready."

"Ready? To do what?"

William reaches down and pats the pistol resting next to him on the seat. "Whatever I have to."

Gradually, the Eddy family adjusts to the travel routine enabling them to truly appreciate the beauty of their environment. Eleanor's fears subside as she makes her adjustments to a new set of domestic responsibilities. During the day she entertains and cares for the children inside the wagon and after they stop for the day she focuses on making the family meal. The evenings are warm, so her only concern is the fire over which she cooks the meal. A few nights are spent in the company of another wagon or two of travelers camping for the night. This is particularly pleasurable for Eleanor because it provides them with an additional degree of security and a form of social companionship.

The travelers they encounter are not only welcomed socially but they provide them with an opportunity to learn of the upcoming conditions on the trail and the progress of the wagon company ahead. An occasional encounter with Indians produces no threat, so Eleanor begins to accept their presence on the trail as a matter of fact. This is not to suggest that there were no problems to overcome. Streams had to be crossed, rain halted their progress for hours at a time, adjustments and repairs to the wagon had to be made, and time for the livestock to graze stalled them periodically. On one occasion, attention to an illness by both children robbed them of any travel time for a day and a half. But, by and large, the information they receive through chance encounters with others suggests that they are on schedule.

Each night William does his best to determine their location on the map relative to what he guessed would be the location of the large group. By his best calculations, and with the aid of information received from others along the trail, he estimated that they would catch up on or around the first of the month.

Much of Eleanor's "free" time is spent keeping the promise she made to her mother to "record as best you can as much as possible of all that happens on your trip." Her mother promised to keep her own personal journal to record her thoughts as well in the hope that it would keep them close in mind and spirit at least, even though they both knew there would be long passages of time before their words could reach each other (if at all). Eleanor's focus on the flora and fauna, and her attempt to describe them, both challenged and excited her. In addition, she found that there was actually some joy and humor to be found in her attempt to explain and describe some of the new duties for which she was now responsible: cooking over an open fire, washing dishes and clothes in buckets, mending clothes while on the move, keeping the children entertained in the confinement of the moving wagon, or taking the reins while William completed his necessary chores outside the wagon.

May 1 –

I think you would be proud of me mother in the way I have adapted to my new life. The whole idea of moving terrified me at first but I surprise even myself at how accustomed I am becoming to the little things I did not think I could handle. Perhaps it is the result of how I know I must appear for the children's sake. But the truth is that I am honestly excited by all the wonderful things I see. I wish you could share these moments with us.

Enough about my feelings. We've now been on the trail for half a month. Our progress goes well although we had hoped to meet the others by this date in May. We have heard that their progress has not gone as well as they had planned either. Independence is the last town where travelers can replenish their supplies before they begin the long drive across the Indian territory. From all we've been told by fellow travelers it is certainly a frontier town, inhabited by people of all classes, many uncivilized and driven by greed. From the best information we can get it appears that we are about a week away from it.

It is time for sleep –

It is on the afternoon of the sixth of May when a rider appears on the trail ahead moving toward them. He stops a short distance away under the shade of a tree and waits for their wagon to approach.

"Hello the wagon! Would you be the Eddy family?"

"Yes, we are," answers William. "And you, sir?"

"Name's Elliott. Milt Elliott. Mr. Reed sent me to find your location."

"So, we're close?" asks William.

"Maybe another day and the rest of this one from our bunch. They figure they're about four days out."

"That's good news," says William. "We're mighty anxious for company."

Milt continues. "Has your trip gone well? Any trouble?"

"Couple 'a small problems, but easier than we expected," answers William. "We were gettin' worried. I know Mr. Reed said he hoped to be in Independence by the first of the month."

Eleanor joins the conversation. "Could we offer you something, Mr. Elliott?"

"Don't want to slow you folks down. I'll ride along for a ways if you don't mind."

"Pleased to have you join us, Mr. Elliott. You'd be most welcome for dinner."

"Mighty nice 'a you, but I think I'd better get back while there's still light. Folks up ahead said to say they's lookin' forward to seein' you."

William continues. "No more so than my family 'n me lookin' forward to sittin' around a campfire with all 'a you. Does it look like everthin's close to the schedule Mr. Reed planned?"

"Couple 'a days behind maybe, but nothin' serious. From what we've learned the larger companies might be leavin' Independence before we get there, but it shouldn't be a problem catchin' 'em."

After the brief visit with Mr. Reed's employee, Eleanor and William's spirits soar in anticipation of what was ahead of them. They traveled an additional hour that evening and spent a joyous time telling stories to their children after supper by the fire. Afterwards, both found it difficult to sleep, so they rose early and were underway before the first light of day. And a wonderful day it was, filled with anticipation and excitement! They eagerly search the trail ahead for any movement as they travel. Telltale signs of the recent passage of livestock further indicate to them that they were drawing close. And then, at a place where the trail broadened into an open meadow, they see the remnants of what was obviously a campsite from the night before, and they become almost giddy.

Still-warm coals provide clear evidence that their meeting is indeed imminent. After a brief discussion, they decide to forego their break and move along as quickly as possible. In a little less than two hours the sounds of moving wagons and livestock can be heard. It is decided that William should ride ahead and announce their presence. He gives the reins to Eleanor, mounts his horse and disappears. Within the hour he returns in the company of James Reed and Milt Elliott.

Mr. Reed is the first to speak. "Welcome, Mrs. Eddy! Milt reported your location and we've been on the lookout for you all day."

Somewhat embarrassed, but more than happy to receive the greeting, she replies, "Thank you, Mr. Reed. We're so pleased to join you. It's nice to see you Mr. Elliott."

"Thank you, ma'am," answers Elliott.

Mr. Reed is quick to add a personal touch. "We're anxious to spend time with you and your family around the fire tonight. Our womenfolk are particularly looking forward to renewing their brief acquaintance with you."

In a short time the Eddy's had caught up with the original group that had passed through Belleville. There is a brief welcome, but there is also a sense of urgency to continue to move ahead. The goal is to catch up with the large company under the leadership of Colonel W. H. Russell. It is made up of several companies, each formed at the beginning of the trek or as a result of differences of opinion or minor arguments that led to smaller group alliances. Word had come down that they had left Independence and the train numbered better than two-hundred wagons and was as long as two miles in length. Since they were still days away from Independence, there is a desire to hurry along so that they can soon join them and eventually become part of an even bigger train headed for Oregon and California. Each company is presided over by a leader selected by the group in a democratic manner. It was his duty to conduct meetings, decide where they would camp each night, and see to it that their rules were enforced. Joined together, the even larger company would make for greater security and a superior internal support.

The journey from this point on is particularly enjoyable for the Eddy family. They are in the company of others and the feeling of belonging to something important was theirs to savor. The party rises early, travels longer hours, and works hard after they stop for the day. Still, there is adequate time each night for the members to gather around the fire and spend a social hour singing, dancing, and telling stories.

Each day Eleanor does her best to become a part of the group by learning all she can of her fellow travelers. At night she faithfully records the information she has gleaned along with the impressions she has formed in an ever-growing letter to her mother.

May 10 -

We have now joined the three original families that left Springfield. Mr. Reed and his wife Margaret have been most kind to us and were largely responsible for our decision to head west. Margaret is an invalid, but her husband takes good care of her. Margaret's mother is also with them. She has been quite ill from the beginning of their trip. Margaret has a daughter who is 12 years old I think named Virginia from her first marriage and three with Mr. Reed. They have three wagons, three teamsters, and two hired help. One of their wagons is the most beautiful I've ever seen. It is truly a home on wheels with every convenience one could imagine. Some say Mr. Reed is of noble blood, born in Ireland and brought here as a boy. He was very wealthy and highly respected back home.

Another family who welcomed us is the George Donner family. He is 62 years of age and a highly respected man who was a prosperous farmer back in Illinois. His wife is Tamsen, a small woman of considerable energy and his second wife. They have three wagons, three young children, and two older ones from his first marriage. They are very nice to us and are willing to give help to anyone who needs it.

The third family that started the trip in Springfield is the Jacob Donner family. He is a brother to George Donner and three years older. His wife is Elizabeth. They have five children, the oldest being about eight. Elizabeth's two boys from an earlier marriage are abut 13 and 11 I think. From what I hear, George Donner's second wife – Tamsen is his third – was Mrs. Jacob Donner's sister. Jacob is much more frail than his brother so they remain quiet at night and more private than the others. They have three wagons also. There are five teamsters who take care of the six Donner wagons and livestock.

The time passes quickly. They arrive in Independence by the eleventh of May and do not stay long. After camping outside town, and entering it only to replenish a few needed supplies, they are ready to be on the move again, especially after hearing that a large company of wagons commanded by Colonel Russell was waiting for latecomers at Wakarusa Creek in Kansas.

It was a prestigious company that included several well-known men. Its leader, Colonel William Russell from Kentucky, had spent several years as secretary to Henry Clay before moving to Missouri and entering the political scene on his own. His reputation as a master orator was known far and wide. Also part of this company was Jessy Quinn Thornton, an attorney from Quincy, Illinois who numbered among his friends such dignitaries as Stephen A. Douglas and Thomas Hart Benton, the major proponent of Manifest Destiny. There was Lillburn Boggs, the former governor of Missouri whose second wife was the granddaughter of Daniel Boone. Also, among the group was Edwin Bryant, the former editor of a newspaper in Louisville, Kentucky. Clearly, the company was highly selective in whom they allowed to join.

By the time they reach the Wakarusa, however, they find that the large company has already departed. Eager to gain protection in Indian Territory they hurry along and manage to catch up with them at a site known as Soldier Creek. There, they petitioned to join the Russell Company and had their request granted. With the addition of this new group of travelers the Russell contingent grew to 72 wagons, 130 men, 65 women, and 125 children, seemingly a large enough company to be secure from attacks by hostile Indians.

May 19 -

We caught up with the Russell Company last night. The Donners and Mr. Reed met with Mr. Russell and we were allowed to join. It is a great relief to have such a large number of wagons and people. We've not had any problems from Indians yet. I shall do my best to meet the new families and help in any way I can...

May 22 -

The men hunt each day so there is plenty of fresh meat. The children are delightful and well behaved. The women seem nice and have kindly taken us into their group. Each night the wagons are drawn into a circle and chained together as a protection against an Indian attack. The livestock are turned out to graze under heavy guard while the women prepare the meals. Most consider such precautions unnecessary since we've had no trouble so far. Travel during these days with the large company have been very pleasant...

May 24 -

The weather has become our biggest hindrance. It rained solidly for two days making travel almost impossible and the crossing of streams and rivers dangerous. The men spend long hours building rafts, taking care of the animals, and keeping the wagons moving through deep mud. Tempers do flare on occasion. Still, spirits remain high in the face of these difficulties because we do manage to make progress...

May 28 –

When we reached the Big Blue River the rains have made it impossible to cross so we've been stalled for days...

May 29 -

A loss of life last night. Margaret Reed's mother died. She had been sick almost from the start but the family gave her the best of care under the conditions they faced. A service was conducted by a minister from our group. She was buried near a beautiful oak tree. A gloom sits over the camp tonight...

A different kind of problem now faced the emigrants. Rain continued to fall, as did the patience of the travelers. Cooperation, it was discovered, had its limits. While some were benefited by the work of the many, others found it to be a hindrance to their progress. Their ox-teams were faster, their wagons and equipment were superior, and their patience with the travelers they began to consider inept was rapidly wearing thin. Quarrels occurred more frequently, and new group alliances began to form.

Creek crossings were the major irritant. Each wagon at every crossing required a group effort, slowing everyone. Heavy rains fell again, and again they were stalled, which led to further frustration. Fortunately for everyone, conditions began to change when they reached the Nebraska River. It was shallow, running across land that was flat. The woods that were so familiar to them back at home were now being replaced by land that was populated by cactus and sagebrush. Their environment was becoming wide-open, devoid of trees, hills, and colorful flora.

By the second of June the journey resumed in earnest, minus twenty wagons that were asked to leave due to petty quarrels. The large company continued under the leadership of Colonel Russell. A change in the landscape was viewed by most as a pleasant relief, and the vast prairie that lay before them was seen as a thing of beauty. Green grass was plentiful, and although the absence of trees made for a shortage of wood, there were still groves of trees to be found along the streams. Buffalo chips were readily available and served as an adequate substitute for firewood in camp.

As they traveled, the soggy conditions of the earlier going slowly began to change to something equally difficult – trail dust. Dry air contributed to firmer ground, but the steady pounding by livestock and wagons soon sent clouds of dust wafting upward to foul eyes, nose, and throat. The dry conditions also took its toll on the wagons, particularly the wheels, causing the wood in them to shrink, become wobbly, and loosen. Eddy spent long hours helping to repair the damage that was the result.

June 12 –

If only I had the words to convey my feelings, Mother. The land is both beautiful and cruel and ever changing, and it is always beyond my ability to describe. The emotions a sunrise or a sun dropping between mountaintops in the distance can create an inner peace I've never felt before. But the awful winds and storm clouds that moved quickly toward us just a short time ago darkening everything caused me to feel a kind of fear I'd not known at home. I wish I could explain...

June 14 –

Today marks the end of our second month on the trail. I think of you every day...

June 16 –

We have reached the point where the north and south branches of the Platte River come together and it was decided that we would camp here for a few days to give everyone a chance to rest. Still, I have much to do but it must not interfere with my letters to you. We often meet people who are returning to the east. I have twice found someone who was willing to carry my letters as far as Independence and mail them for me. Still there is no telling how long it will take for them to reach you.

It is hard for me to explain exactly where we are. The women are seldom brought in to the discussions and planning which remain the domain of our men. As I understand it, our trail will follow close to the North Platte River and we are heading toward Ft. Laramie...

June 22 –

Our pace has quickened but the problems this new land has created make time seem to stand still. The rain stopped days ago and now we are moving through prairies that have lost the beauty we first saw. Two weeks ago I said I hoped it would never rain again. Now the dry air, the dust, and the heat during the day have made me long for more drops from heaven. My strength and my will seem to be slowly fading as we go through our daily routine. I do not know how my darling William can do all he is asked to do. Not only does he take care of us but each night and many times during the day he is asked to help someone solve a problem with his wagon. And still he takes his turn with the other men...

July 1 -

I wish I could say we all are bearing up well under our hardships but it would not be true. Most are exhausted.

Illnesses of all kinds continue to plague us all. The alkali
water has caused diarrhea for most and we live in dust.

This must sound terrible, mother. Please do not worry or
think I'm weak. My children have not seen anything but a
happy and loving mother. A gift I know I received from you
every day of my life...

Even before the company reached the North Platte, anger and
frustration had reached its boiling point. Colonel Russell was removed as
leader and replaced by Lillburn Boggs. This, in turn, resulted in the
formations of several splinter groups, each in need of its own identity as
they continued their movement toward Little Sandy Creek.

On the eleventh of July they had reached a site known as
Independence Rock. It was clear to everyone that they were only a third
of the way to their destination in California and many were becoming
anxious about the fact that they were falling behind.

By this time the name Lansford Hastings had become known to
all the emigrants. His letter *Emigrants' Guide to Oregon and California*
was the inspiration for many travelers' decision to move west. His view,
supported by personal experience, was that the new road he proposed
was superior to the one most were following on the Established
California Trail to Ft. Hall. It was, he claimed, much shorter with a good
supply of wood, water, and grass for the livestock. He did acknowledge
that there was one difficult stretch of some forty miles that experienced
travelers would handle with ease.

It also was apparent to all that a decision as to which trail they
would follow had to be made soon because at Little Sandy Creek the trail
forked, one leading to the Established California Trail and the other
toward Fort Bridger, the shortcut advocated by Hastings.

3

A FORK IN THE TRAIL

Over a small fire, a steaming pot hangs suspended. Nearby, seated beside their wagon, Eleanor pores over the contents of a small box. She gently lifts one treasure after another for a closer examination: a dried flower, a lace handkerchief, a broach of carved ivory, a stack of letters tied together, and a small bottle of perfume. She opens the bottle and brings it to her nose.

Finally, she removes a family photograph in which she and her sister stand next to her mother and father, seated between them. Reverently, she places the tips of her fingers on the pair. Next to her near the wagon, James plays in the dirt near the crude cradle that holds his one-year-old sleeping sister.

A movement in the distance captures her attention. She looks up and sees her husband striding confidently toward her. She closes the box and sets it behind her.

Even before he arrives, William announces: "It's settled!"

Eleanor waits for him to close the distance and squat next to her before she responds. "What?"

"The trail we'll follow – the people we'll be travelin' with." He waits for her reaction. When there is none he reaches out to lift the top of the pot to look inside. Then he continues. "We leave at dawn. There was lots of arguin' but we finally settled on the Hastings' cutoff."

"So, Mr. Hastings will be the guide?"

"That was part 'a the problem. He's gone on to Fort Bridger with another party. But he left word that he'd meet us there and take us through."

A crease appears in Eleanor's brow. "Is it safe?"

"Reed and the Donners think so. In the long run it'll save the ones 'a us that's goin' to California several hundred miles."

"Then what was the arguin' all about?"

"Well, for one thing a feller who'd just come back from California with Hastings said it was shorter but too dangerous."

"Then?"

"Most didn't pay him much mind," says William. "The main thing that convinced the group was the time it would save us. The claim is that the weather could be a real problem. We'd be the last bunch 'a wagons headin' to California, so any time we could save could be mighty important."

"So everybody's goin' that way?"

"No. The bigger company's decided to head north to Fort Hall and pick up the California Trail."

"Then why aren't we? Seems to make sense to stay with the larger companies. Safer, too."

"But they move slower, and time's gettin' short."

Eleanor remains quiet for several seconds before she gets a plate and goes to the pot. She puts a scoop of its contents on the plate and then fishes out a piece of meat to set on top. As soon as she hands it to William, Jimmy squats next to his father and Eleanor prepares a bowl for him. Clearly not convinced that the right decision has been made, she pursues her inquiry. "Did the man say why it was dangerous?"

"Said it was too narrow for wagons."

"Isn't that important? He'd know wouldn't he? Who was he?"

"Mountain man," answers William. "Pretty scruffy trapper whose words didn't hold much weight with the group. Claimed he couldn't know nothin' 'bout wagons, livin' the way he does. He and Reed did most of the arguin.'"

"Don't you think we should –"

William interrupts. "Already decided. Case was made that time is everythin'. We still got the toughest part'a the trip ahead of us. There's already ice on the water buckets in the mornin', 'n it's still July."

Unconvinced, Eleanor continues. "Then why are the others taking the other way? Isn't the safer way more important?"

"We've done pretty well so far, ain't we?"

Eleanor looks over her shoulder at the mountains to the west just as the sun comes to rest on top of a peak. "Wasn't nothing like that."

William looks up and offers a reassuring smile. "This doesn't sound like you, Mrs. Eddy. Ain't complained yet."

"Not complainin' now. Just want to know we're making the right choice."

The tone of William's voice changes. He speaks slowly and more softly. "I know how hard this has been for you, Ellie, but it's all gonna' be worth it. Just wait 'n see."

"I believe you. I was just ... comfortable where we were. And the kids are ..."

"I know this is all my idea. But I'm doin' it fer all'a us. I know you'll love it."

"Who's to be the leader?' asks Eleanor.

"Ain't picked 'em yet. We'll get to it when we camp tomorrow night."

"Mr. Reed?"

"Not likely."

"Why not? He's certainly a gentleman. A man of property."

"He is that," answers William, "but some 'a the men hold him as a bit too fancy. Says he feels he's better'n the rest. Used words like 'aristocratic' 'n 'blueblood'."

"Oh, I don't think that's true."

"It's not true. But that's the way they feel. Just jealous, if you ask me. Much more likely to be George Donner. All the men respect him, 'n he's sure done his share 'a travelin'. Mighty prosperous, too."

July 17 –

It has been decided that we will take a shorter route. That means we will leave the large company now led by Mr. Boggs. William says there are several people who have asked to be a part of our group. The largest family to join us is the Murphy clan. A widow named Lavina is the leader. There are 13 of them. Seven are her children. Five range in age from 10 to about 15. Her two married daughters (Sarah and Harriet) and their families are also with her. Sarah is married to William Foster and they have one boy. Harriet is married to William Pike. They have two daughters. Lavina is from Tennessee and she knew our friends the Stewarts from Belleville. She moved to Missouri after she lost her husband. The family all seem nice and helpful to all...

July 18 –

An Irish family joined us at Little Sandy Creek. Their name is Breen. They are a welcome addition. Patrick and Margaret have seven children. One is still a baby and the oldest is about 15. Patrick was born in Ireland. After becoming an American he became a farmer. William likes him very much but he stayed away from his wife who he says is too bossy. They seem to be very prosperous. They have three wagons, several oxen, horses, and milk cows. They are private folks. Most of the time they choose to remain with their family group...

July 19 –

Another family, the Kesebergs, asked to join us this morning.. He is German. His wife is Philippine. They have two small children. Traveling with them is an older man named Hardcoop and a teamster by the name of Karl Burger. William says there is bad blood between Mr. Reed and Keseberg. It has something to do with an accusation Mr. Reed made against him for robbing Indian graves. There are also rumors that he beats his wife.

Two other men, partners they say – Joseph Reinhardt and Augustus Spitzer –are both German and about 30 years old. And there is another German couple named Wolfinger. They are about 30. Her name is Doris, but no one knows his first name. He just goes by Wolfinger.

On the nineteenth of July, a Sunday, the Boggs Company made its last full camp together at Little Sandy Creek. The next day they would take the Greenwood cutoff while the Reed-Donner group would head south to Ft. Bridger.

July 20 –

Many tearful farewells today when the members of the Boggs Company left camp. The sorrow quickly changed to a general spirit of excitement at the thought of beginning a shorter and better route. It is difficult to know exactly how many members of our new party there are. At the meeting of the new group George Donner was elected leader. My best count of our fellow travelers is now 71...

The next day the newly named Donner Party make little progress as they find the traveling difficult down the Little Sandy River. Some of the livestock are sick or dying as a result of the alkali tainted water and it slows their progress. The remainder of the trip is not easy but after a long drive of eighteen miles they pull into Ft. Bridger, which consists of two cabins at the end of a large corral. It is situated in a beautiful meadow near the Green River. The river is clear and cold and a welcome sight to the weary travelers. It is the twenty-seventh of July.

The door to one of the cabins opens and several men exit and walk toward the camp where the Donner Party settlers are gathered around a large fire, talking quietly. The men, with the exception of George Donner, join their family group and squat or sit. Donner moves to a position just outside the circle of emigrants, and everyone adjusts their position in order to face him.

Before he can speak, his wife, Tamsen, sitting on a log near the fire breaks the silence with, "What is the situation, Mr. Donner?"

Donner does not respond immediately, as though searching for the correct way to proceed. Finally: "Mr. Hastings isn't here."

His wife continues. "Why not? Where is he?"

"He left with a party of sixty wagons five days ago."

Tamsen continues her search for answers. "It was my understanding that he was to meet us here!"

"Mine as well. He did leave directions for us to follow. Mr. Bridger said the other folks didn't feel they could wait any longer. The season is getting late."

Lewis Keseberg is quick to follow up on the interrogation. "How can you trust what Bridger says, or Hastings' directions for that matter?"

Reed attempts to offer his support of Donner. "What choice do we have, Mr. Keseberg?"

Keseberg turns and glares at Reed. "At this stage, not much I reckon. We're here due mainly to the urging of you and Donner. You'd better be right."

In a calm voice, Reed replies, "You were free to do what you wanted at any time."

34

"Hastings' Cutoff was your choice, Reed! We were promised lots of things. No danger from Indians. A good trail with no canyons to cross. Plenty of grass and water."

"You know we were told there was one stretch of forty miles of dry travel," explains Reed.

"That we can handle," argues Keseberg, "we were told Hastings would be here to guide us. Where is he?"

"I told you," answers Donner. "He's guiding a company of wagons along his trail."

"And where does that leave us?" questions Keseberg.

Scattered mumblings of concurrence occur from the group. Donner watches and listens in an attempt to discover the mood of the group. "Hold on. You all had a vote. We chose the cutoff for good reasons. Best thing now is to get a good night's rest. The earlier we leave the better the chance of catching up with the other party."

Instead, they halted for four days, mainly to make a few necessary repairs and to give the livestock a chance to graze. Also, there was reluctance on the part of the group to begin without Hastings being present. George Donner hired a new driver by the name of Jean Baptise, and Reed replaced the oxen he had lost to bad water.

July 28 -

Another family has decided to join us. William and Amanda McCutcheon from Missouri. They have a year old baby. William is a very powerful man who stands well over six feet tall. My William reports that he is friendly and always willing to help. Before joining us they had traveled with another wagon that broke down. I think they have made an arrangement to travel with another family...

35

The emigrants begin to grow impatient and nervous about their lack of progress. It is decided that they should continue without the leadership of Hastings. So on the last day of July the Donner Party pulls away from Ft. Bridger. In a short while they are in country that makes for very rough traveling. Due to the scarcity of travel on the road the trail has not been beaten down and easy to follow. They are forced to travel close to towering cliffs that present more dangers than they had yet encountered.

On horseback, George Donner, James Reed, and Patrick Breen have gone ahead to examine Hastings' recommended route. Breen, riding in the lead, catches sight of something and slows his pace. He slowly advances and dismounts. Placed in a conspicuous position at the top of a bush next to the trail is a letter. Breen plucks it from its resting place and walks back to his companions.

An hour later back in camp the members of the Donner Party sit or stand around the fire waiting to hear the news as reported by the scouting party. George Donner, holding the letter, waits for quiet before he reads:

To any who are following this trail I would advise against following it from this point on. It is possible that our own party may not get through. It would be best to make camp and send a messenger ahead to overtake me. I will return and guide you across the mountains by a better and shorter route.

Lansford Hastings

Keseberg is quick to voice his complaint: "Goddamn Hastings! Why didn't he tell us this before?"

In a calm voice, Breen seeks Donner's counsel. "What do we do now, George?"

Reed provides the answer. "He told us what to do."

Donner adds, "Some of us will have to go ahead and bring him back."

"I'll go," volunteers Reed.

"And what do the rest of us do? Sit here 'n wait?" asks Keseberg sarcastically.

"We've plenty to do," offers Donner in an attempt to calm the fears of the group. "All of us need the time for repairs. It may be a blessing."

Seeking the support of the group, Keseberg continues. "We shoulda' took the trail to Ft. Hall."

"But we didn't!" answers Reed, his anger rising.

In a conciliatory tone, Donner offers his advice. "Makes no sense to backtrack now. That'd just lose us time and we'd still have the long way left to us. We'd never make it across the mountains in time."

William McCutcheon, a brute of a man with a full black beard, rises from his kneeling position. "I'll go along with Mr. Reed."

"Thanks, Bill," says Reed.

Charles Stanton, a diminutive but strong and wiry bachelor, stands next to McCutcheon. "Count me in." The contrast between the comparative size of the two volunteers is almost comic, but his willingness to do his part is quickly accepted by the group. Without wasting any time the three volunteers are on their horses and moving ahead in the canyon. It is the sixth of August.

Everyone expected a quick return by the three men, so after four days passed without a word from them, a near panic developed. On the evening of the fifth day a meeting of the men was held to decide their course of action.

Breen is the first to speak. "*Five days*, Mr. Donner What are we to think?"

"I admit it's bad," answers Donner, "but what can we do?"

37

Keseberg is quick to respond. "Go ahead of course! If we just sit here, we'll die."

"Go ahead in what direction? We've been warned of the dangers to come."

Eddy raises another issue. "What about our food supply?"

Donner shakes his head. "You know very well. It's low."

Eddy continues, "Do we have enough time before it snows?"

"I'll answer that," says Keseberg. "Every night the cold grows more fierce. It won't be long before it's too late."

Patrick Dolan rises to get a log to throw on the fire. "Mr. Donner, it seems to me we have to do somthin'. We may not be frontiersmen, but we's use to hard work. Nothin's worse than just sittin' here."

Donner gives him his full attention. "By my count, we have no more than twenty men to break trail ... to keep the wagons movin' ... to take care of the cattle. We must have a direction to –"

Everyone's attention is suddenly drawn to a sound across the stream. Through the trees appears a single rider, slumped over and barely hanging on. It is James Reed.

Two of the men bound across the shallow creek. One takes the reins of the exhausted horse as the other helps to steady Reed in the saddle. The men quickly gather around as Reed dismounts and crumbles in a heap.

An hour later the settlers are gathered around Reed as he chews on a piece of jerky and drinks a cup of dark coffee.

"It took the three of us two days just to get out of the Wahsatch," says Reed. "Hastings was right to warn us against the river trail. The canyons are so narrow a wagon can barely fit through. One had crashed down a mountainside into nothin' but splinters below."

"Then why in hell did he want us to follow him?" asks Keseberg.

"Wouldn't say," says Reed. "Refused to ride all the way back with us. Claimed he had to stay with his party and get 'em across the dry part."

Bill Foster slams down a shovel he was holding. "Good thing he didn't. Might 'a got his head busted!"

"He did come part way and sketched out an alternate route," explains Reed. "I tried to follow it on the way back, so I think I got it right. I marked it with blazes as I went along."

"What happened to the other two men?" asks Donner.

"Their horses gave out – mine, too. Had to borrow one from Hastings. Said they'd be waitin' for us."

"All of us here are ready to travel, says Donner. "You up to it at first light, Jim?"

"I will be."

Foster, still angry, turns and walks toward his wagon. "Sure lookin' forward to runnin' into that bastard Hastings one a' these days."

August 13 –

It has been mostly trouble since I last sat down to write. Mr. Reed found Hastings and he mapped out another trail for us to follow. It has been hard going ever since. There seems to be no easy way for us to travel. Our poor men spend a good part of every day hacking their way through a tangle of dense brush and cutting down aspens and willow trees. They work until they almost drop and their hands are bloody...

August 14 –

If anything, the work grows more difficult for the men. There are not enough of them to do everything that needs doing. They had to double the teams of oxen and use windlasses to make it over many ridges. They have to pile dirt and brush on both sides of the boulders that are too big to be moved. They cut small trees and brush and throw shovelfuls of dirt on top for the wagons to move. It's awful. I don't know how they can hold up under such a strain... The tempers grow shorter by the hour. I fear for our well-being...

August 15

A miracle. This afternoon three wagons joined us. A welcome surprise for all! 13 new members added to our company. They are led by Franklin Graves (all their folks call him Uncle Billy). He is an older man who was a farmer in Illinois. His wife is Elizabeth. They have nine children. Their oldest daughter is Sarah and her husband is James Fosdick. The rest of the children range from the oldest (Mary, 20) to the youngest, a one-year old little girl. With them is their teamster, John Snyder. They told us they had left their company in Laramie and traveled alone to Ft. Bridger where they heard of the Donners. That's when they decided to join us. Four new men to help create a trail! They are sorely needed...

Even with the addition of the new men, the agony went on day after day for more than two weeks. Some days they were lucky to make even a mile. Stanton and McCutcheon were still lost, and of the men left, four or five were too sick or old to be of any help. Their party numbered eighty-seven, of which fifty-seven were women and children. At the top of some ridges they could see the wide valley of the Great Salt Lake. So close - yet so far away.

August 28 –

The two lost men stumbled into camp last night more dead than alive. Our joy soon turned to near panic as they told us we had to cross a range of mountains far worse than the ones we'd just managed. At first it seemed enough to break what spirit was left in the men. But there was no choice but to go on...

August 31 –

We made it! But it is the end of August. It has taken us nearly a month to travel 38 miles. Time is winning the real battle...

4

THE DESERT DRIVE

L ittle did they know the battle had just begun – but it would be with one less member. Luke Halloran, a twenty-five year-old consumptive died at the edge of the Great Salt Lake Plain and was buried before they confronted their next challenge. The group now known as the Donner Party numbered eighty-six.

The next day the wagons pushed on without taking a day to recover. They had pleasant going for a while, but one of Reed's wagons broke an axle and they had to go fifteen miles to find wood out of which they could cut another. The following day was even hotter as they moved across a dry plain of sage-brush. By the end of the day they reached a meadow in which there was a fine spring.

Reed is the first to notice a signpost sticking out of the ground. It is another message from Hastings that reads, "2 days – 2 nights – hard drive." Eddy's reaction speaks for all the emigrants: "The lying bastard said thirty-five or forty miles at the most. It's probably more'n twice that."

It is decided that the next day should be spent preparing and relaxing. It would give the livestock time to rest, graze, and drink their fill. Every receptacle the people can find is filled with water, and food is prepared so it can be eaten as they travel.

By dawn of the third day they move out. Hastings' trail is nothing more than wheel marks. It leads them across a great open valley toward a range of high hills. When they arrive they are discouraged to find that they still must maneuver a steep hill that leads to a pass that rises a good thousand feet.

When they reach the top and can look out and see what is ahead of them their spirits plummet. After another steep descent is another plain much like the one they had just crossed. Rocky hills in the distance signal no chance for water. Then, over the top of these volcanic hills they can see a great salt plain, clearly more than forty miles of desert.

September 3 –

We managed to get down the steep hill by nightfall. Our water supply is very low, so the animals cannot be given more than what is necessary to keep them alive. With a heavy moon above to give us enough light it was decided to move ahead for at least a few miles. The burning heat of the day has changed to a terrible chill. We have stopped for a brief rest and I am writing this now because I am, like most, too tired to sleep...

September 4 –

I am trying my best mother to keep my thoughts straight. Our wagons took a terrible beating coming down the hill. The oxen are exhausted but no more so than the rest of us. The wagons have begun to separate. Ours along with the Graves have taken the lead but no matter how fast we move the mountains ahead seem an impossible distance away...

September 5 –

If ever this reaches you I know how hard it will be to read. The suffering is beyond description. The cattle have run free because the wagons had to spread out for fear of getting stuck in the tracks of others. The wheels break through the thin crust and sink into the wet salt water below. Most of us set out on foot. How we made it through this awful night I'll never know...

September 6 –

When we went back to recover our belongings it was worse than we had feared. The bigger wagons had broken through the crust and the oxen could pull them no farther. Reed lost two. We put our team to his last one, and Pike put his team to ours. As I sit here now I know our fate hangs in the balance. The hardest part of the journey lies ahead. May God look over us...

Three days and three nights have been spent in the desert and there is still no end in sight. The wagons are widely scattered and contact with others is almost hopeless. A few have gone ahead but the heavier wagons of Reed and Donner lag far behind. Without water, the oxen are rendered helpless and even the emigrants recognize that they might die of thirst if they do not find water soon. Reed decides to go ahead in search of water and return after he has found some. He travels almost thirty miles on his horse before he comes upon some willows that surround a spring. Eddy and a few emigrants are already there. He rests for only a short while before starting back with a pail of water to keep his family alive.

September 7 –

Another awful night. We had to abandon our wagon and drive the oxen on to find water. The Graves family made it here with us, but we have lost the others. Mr. Reed rode in later and stayed long enough to rest his horse and get a bucket of water to take with him...

September 11 –

I was not sure I would even be alive to continue my writing. We did make it across somehow and have made camp in a small meadow that has water. Mr. Reed decided to abandon his big wagon because he didn't have enough oxen to pull it. My William offered to lend his oxen to Mr. Reed and share it with him. Then he loaned our wagon to Mr. Pike. Everyone in our party is on edge and there has been much bickering...

Somehow everyone manages to make it across the desert after six days of continuous struggle. The next day is spent searching for their cattle and missing oxen. Everyone knows that if most cannot be found it would be a catastrophe. The fear is that they have either been killed by Indians or have died of thirst.

The next morning members of the party huddle around a campfire. The women do their best to prepare a meal. The children, wrapped in blankets, sit quietly or sleep. Five men, (Keseberg, Eddy, Breen, George Donner, and his brother, Jacob) smoke their pipes in front of the fire.

Jacob Donner, his body wracked with pain, does his best to take stock of their condition. "I make it out to be thirty-six oxen gone. There's no tellin' just how many cattle are missing, but I put it at around fifty."

"Some of the men left before sun-up for one last look," says Eddy.

Breen adds his thought. "It's not likely they'll find any with all the Indians out there."

"What we got left is a mighty sorry lookin' lot," adds Keseberg.

"At least the folks all got across," says Eddy.

"Hard to say if we got enough supplies to carry us through," warns George Donner. "We need to find game."

Eddy adds his concern. "The wagons need lots 'a work."

"They sure do, but we got to get on the trail."

"What about the Reeds?" asks Eddy.

"Graves and Breen said they'd loan him an ox," answers George Donner. "Along with yours, he should get through."

Keseberg sneers, "I lost one, and I'm still carrying some 'a his supplies in my wagon."

"Sure, for a share of it," answers Eddy.

"I'm not the only one. Besides, why should I carry *his* goods for nothin'? He's the one who got us here."

"Don't forget that goddamn Hastings!" adds Breen.

George Donner attempts to change the focus of their conversation. "Gentlemen, I suggest we put these feelings aside and deal with more immediate problems. I propose we leave at sun-up tomorrow."

"What if the men aren't back?" asks Eddy.

"They'll catch up."

Keseberg is quick to agree. "Makes sense to me to get movin'. Don't like these cold mornings."

"Any objections from any 'a you?" asks George Donner. Each man responds by shaking his head. "Good. Let's pass the word along. Sun-up tomorrow."

Along a mountain trail nineteen wagons follow wheel tracks along the base of a mountain range that rises out of the desert. It is snowing. A few have a cow under yoke. The considerably smaller herd of cattle trudge wearily forward.

Two riders, Milt Elliott, Reed's teamster, and Billy Graves, moving along two cows, approach the train. Several men ride out to meet them.

"All we could find, Mr. Donner," says Billy.

George Donner offers an understanding smile. "At least it's somethin', boys."

"Found another note," says Elliott.

"Hastings?"

"Yep," answers Elliott, "it was at a spring about a mile ahead. Says that beyond that there's another dry stretch of about forty miles."

Jacob Donner's head snaps around. "Forty miles! Jesus, how can we do that, George?"

"I don't know."

At a snail's pace, a smaller segment of the wagon train plods forward through a desolate area at the base of a mountain range. In a dreamlike trance the emigrants walk alongside the wagon or next to the cattle that are little more than skeletons. Three men, Eddy, Breen, and John Snyder, a teamster for the Graves family, walk together next to the Eddy wagon.

"Goddamn Hastings must be crazy," says Snyder. "We follow his trail due south for days, find a gap through the mountains, then back in the same direction we just came. Any damn fool knows California is *west*!"

"The bastard ain't never been on this trail before," adds Breen. We're followin' a goddamned liar."

Eddy changes the subject. "If we could just get a little rest for the livestock and some decent grass, we could –"

"Hell, the grass ain't worth shit!" says Snyder. "Nothin' can live in this God-forsaken country."

Eddy looks to his right. "They do." A hundred yards away, five "Digger" Indians, two of whom are stark naked, stand quietly watching the wagon train pass by.

"They ain't human," says Snyder.

"If they can make it, we can. If we just knew how far we had to go."

Breen adds to this, "The ones we talked to yesterday said we was mighty far away."

"They don't know!" growls Snyder. "They'd say anythin'. They's just lookin' to steal whatever they can get their hands on."

48

"Bad idea to split into two groups," offers Breen.

Eddy explains, "Camping in different spots gives the herd a better chance to graze."

"I know all that, but I still like the safety of all the wagons together."

September 16 –

Endless travel. No one seems to know exactly where we are but we are heading toward the Humbolt River...

On the night of September eighteenth, all members of the Donner Party are gathered around a campfire. George Donner addresses the group.

"Folks, we asked you here to make it clear what we're facing. This is to be our last fresh water for at least a few days. Mr. Pike will be taking Mr. Eddy's wagon. Mr. Reed will use his team. The animals are in bad shape. Our supplies are low. No one knows what's ahead. Sending someone ahead is necessary. If he can get through to Captain Sutter, maybe supplies can be sent back to get us through. It can be dangerous."

"I'll go, Mr. Donner," says Stanton. There is stifled laughter.

"And what's to make a bachelor come back?" asks Keseberg sarcastically.

"My word."

McCutcheon raises his hand. "I'll go with him. Travelin' alone's too risky."

George Donner lets the muffled conversation die down before he speaks. "Folks, these are two honorable men. If anyone can make it, they can. Any Objections?" His words are followed by silence. "It's settled then. We'll be happy to look after your wife and baby, Mr. McCutcheon."

September 24 –

Another problem. We've come into an area belonging to what's known as Digger Indians. They seem friendly enough but they are very poor and have a rugged life. Two of Mr. Donners horses are missing and everyone knows it was the Indians who took them. We have all been on the alert when they are near. Some of them have told our men that we are more than 20 days – what the men guess is 200 miles - to what's called the Humbolt Sink – a swamp in a desert valley...

September 28 –

Two oxen stolen last night and a horse belonging to Uncle Billy. William says the Indians have been shooting arrows at anyone who leaves camp...

September 30 –

We have finally reached the Humboldt River. That means we are back on the main trail to California...

On the fifth of October, the rear section of the wagon train is in the process of climbing a long sand hill. The going is tough enough to require doubling the teams. Two of the Graves' wagons have reached the top and sit waiting while their oxen are being brought back to be used below.

Next in line is the third Graves' wagon, driven by John Snyder. Anxious to make it to the top, he has begun the climb without the aid of another team. When his wheels begin to slide and sink, he angrily resorts to the whip.

Waiting behind is the Reed/Eddy wagon, already having added a yoke of oxen from another wagon. The driver, Milt Elliott, impatient to get moving, pulls his wagon next to Snyder's to pass.

"Goddammit, Elliott, wait your turn!" yells Snyder.

"We're waistin' time," replies Elliott. "I'm already double-yoked."

The way is far too narrow. Elliott's lead yoke becomes tangled with Snyder's team.

"Now look what you done," screams Snyder. "You idiot!"

Elliott jumps down and attempts to untangle the mess. The unruly animals make that impossible. Snyder climbs down, brandishing his bullwhip. He hits an ox in the Elliott team with the handle of the whip.

"Stop that, goddammit!"

"You're the one I should hit!" says Snyder.

"Touch me 'n I'll break your damn neck!"

Reed and his wife approach the men. "What's the problem?"

"Your goddamn driver's the problem!" replies Snyder. "You 'n your wagon can wait your damn turn."

"Keep a civil tongue, Mr. Snyder."

"Go to hell!" yells Snyder. "You're the cause of all our troubles. I should whip you!"

Reed, shocked and angered by these words, pulls his hunting knife from his belt. "Don't you raise your hand to me, Mister!"

Snyder's fury explodes. With the handle of his bullwhip he hits Reed across the head, opening a huge gash. Instinctively, Reed drives the knife upward as the blow is struck. The knife digs deeply into Snyder's chest just below the collarbone.

Margaret Reed steps between the two. Snyder, continuing to lash out, hits Mrs. Reed, knocking her to the ground. Even with the knife embedded deep in his chest, he strikes Reed twice more. The last blow brings Reed to his knees.

Snyder becomes aware of the knife. He staggers backward, blood foaming from his mouth.

Reed, though stunned, now realizes the result of his actions. "Oh, my God!" He rises and moves toward Snyder, who simply stands dumbfounded.

With blood running down his face, Reed extracts the knife and throws it away in disgust. He attempts to support the wounded man as he slumps to the ground.

As Snyder falls, Elliott, young Billy Graves, and Breen rush to his side. Snyder looks up and sees Breen. "Uncle Patrick, I'm dead!"

Virginia Reed joins her mother, now recovered from the blow, at Reed's side and they attempt to minister to his wounds.

Though wounded badly, Reed's only concern is the fallen Snyder. He kneels next to him and pulls himself close. "Forgive, me, John."

"I am to blame, Mr. Reed." answers Snyder. His eyes slowly close.

Elliot, bending over him, looks up, "He's dead, Mr. Reed."

A short while later a group of men who own wagons, along with several of their teamsters, are gathered, apart from the rest of the party.

Keseberg is the first to speak. "Why waste time talking? I say string him up right now. Only way to deal with a murderer."

Breen answers, "It *was* a fight."

"You're takin' Reed's side?"

"I'm not takin' anybody's side. I's just sayin' that it was a fight. Both men were responsible."

"And who's layin' dead, with a knife in his heart?" says Keseberg.

"He had a whip!"

"Hardly a murder weapon," argues Keseberg. "From the beginning, Reed has been responsible for our troubles. Always held himself higher than the rest 'a us."

Breen resumes his defense. "He works as hard as any man here."

"That's not enough to forgive murder! I say we lynch him now!"

The other group consists of Elliott, Eddy, and Reed, being tended to by his daughter, Virginia. Mrs. Reed, her head bandaged, lies on the ground next to them.

Elliott, watching the other group closely, gestures in their direction. "I don't like the looks of that..."

Eddy looks up, assesses the situation and offers his opinion. "We'd best arm ourselves."

All the while, Reed remains unresponsive, but he carefully watches the other group. Eddy goes to the wagon. As he does so, Keseberg and Graves prop a wagon tongue into the air. Keseberg tosses a rope over the top.

After a few minutes of quiet conversation, the lynching party moves toward the other group. The three men from that group are on their feet waiting for them. Each is armed with two double-barreled pistols and a double-barreled shotgun.

Keseberg announces in a loud voice, "We want Reed right now!"

Eddy answers in an equally strong voice: "You go to hell!"

Keseberg responds with an unintelligible German curse. Finally, to be understood by all, "Everybody knows how to handle a murderer."

Eddy is quick to answer. "Everybody's not here. Mr. Reed's men aren't here, and the Donners aren't here to have a say."

"His friends can't protect him now," says Keseberg.

"We can. This was not Mr. Reed's doin'. Besides, it was a fair fight."

"Snyder's dead!" shouts Keseberg.

Eddy responds by pointing at the Reeds. "And look at the condition of the Reeds!"

"They're alive!"

"Enough of this. Any 'a you try to harm him and you just might join Snyder."

The other men look at one another, but offer no response. Keseberg continues his rant. "We intend to have justice. You can't protect him forever."

"Maybe not, but we'll do our damnedest."

"There's only one way out for Reed other than the noose."

For the first time Reed looks up and speaks: "What's that?"

Seeing his opening, Keseberg continues, "Banish him from the group. Send him away without a gun or water."

"Go to hell!" says Reed. "I'll not leave my family."

Eddy counters Keseberg's position. "Without a gun or water? Might as well hang him now."

"It's one or the other," answers Kesebarg.

After a moment of silence, Eddy makes a request: "Give us a few minutes." With a degree of reluctance the vigilantes slowly withdraw, leaving the three men to discuss the choice.

Reed is the first to speak. "I won't leave my family."

"We can look after them," offers Eddy. "You're the one who's in danger, Jim."

"Those men won't –"

Elliott interrupts. "They'll damn sure try. They're mighty serious."

Eddy supports his argument. "Someone's bound to get hurt. There really ain't much of a choice."

"But how could I make it without a gun?" asks Reed.

"One 'a us can sneak out at night and bring you one," says Eddy. "Besides, the Donners are ahead 'a us. They can help."

"All right, but you have to promise you'll take care of my family."

54

"You got my word on it," says Eddy.

"Mine, too," adds Elliott.

It is dawn of the next day. Most of the members of the party are gathered around Snyder's gravesite. The Reeds and their children stand well apart from the group.

After the completion of the crude ceremony the emigrants move toward their wagons in preparation for the continuation of their journey. Keseberg and a few others hesitate to watch as Reed, his head almost covered in bloody bandages, shakes hands with Eddy and Elliott, kisses his wife and crying children, and then mounts his horse. He has little more than the clothes on his back with him. After taking one last look at his wife, Reed slowly rides out of camp.

September 6 –

Mr. Reed was forced to leave camp this morning without anything but his horse. He killed John Snyder after an argument. William says he was innocent and only defending himself and his wife. Several men were threatening to hang him. Mrs. Reed sneaked ahead of the wagons and brought him a gun... What has happened to us?...

By dusk of the same evening the party has set up camp in a particularly bleak spot. Eddy and William Pike enter and walk toward the fire. Each carries a rabbit. They hand their game to one of the women working on the evening meal.

"Looks like pretty slim pickins," says Breen.

"Best we could do," answers Eddy.

Pike adds, "Had arrows shot at us all day."

"Pretty puny shots," says Eddy. "They couldn't get close enough to do any harm. Still, they's a damned nuisance. Found a note from Reed. Said the earlier parties had been under attack by Indians."

"You think McCutcheon and Stanton have reached Sutter yet?" asks Breen.

"It's possible. Two men without wagons can make good time."

"What'a they been gone, two weeks?" asks Elliott.

"More."

"Hell, they's likely dead somewheres," says Breen. "Stuck full 'a arrows."

"Could be," agrees Elliott. "We ain't seen no signs from them along the way."

"'Shit, they ain't followin' this goddamn trail!" complains Breen.

"Hardcoop's missing," says Elliott.

"What?" asks Eddy.

Elliott continues. He was in Keseberg's wagon, but Keseberg said he ain't seen him for several hours."

"Didn't anybody go back to look?" asks Eddy.

"No one would let me use a horse," explains Elliott.

Eddy walks to Keseberg's wagon, a short distance away. Keseberg is working on some equipment. "What happened to Hardcoop?" asks Eddy.

"Why ask me?" says Keseberg. "He's not my responsibility."

"He was riding in your wagon."

"Made him walk like the rest 'a us."

"He's sixty. And sick!"

"If he couldn't keep up, he should never have started. I'm not risking my family for an old man."

"You bastard!"

Eddy turns, finds Franklin Graves sitting by the campfire, and walks directly to him. "Mr. Graves, I need the loan of one of your horses. Hardcoop is somewhere back on the trail."

Graves looks up angrily, "Ain't gonna' kill one 'a my horses for an old man – a damned foreigner who ain't no good to nobody."

"But he –"

"You're not usin' any 'a my horses! Now get away from me!"

Eddy slowly turns and walks back to where Elliott is sitting.

"Any luck?" asks Elliott.

"My God, Milt, what have we become? I'm goin' back a ways to build a bonfire so he can find his way here … if he's still able."

"I'll help."

After hearing of Hardcoop's plight, everyone is asked to help in finding him and everyone refuses. Eddy, Pike and Elliott then volunteer to go back on foot and carry him back to camp. Again everyone refuses to wait for them. Traveling alone through Indian-territory is much too dangerous, so he is left to die. It has now become everyone for himself.

September 7 –

This morning William found the animals too weak to pull Mr. Reeds big wagon so it had to be abandoned. He paid Mr. Graves for the loan of a lighter wagon and then we spent most of the rest of the day moving the Reeds necessary possessions to the new wagon along with a few of our own. We buried the rest…

On the twelfth of September the rear section of the wagon train, consisting of eleven wagons, catches up with the front section, of which there are five. George and Jacob Donner walk out to meet the wagons as they approach. Eddy and Breen are the first to greet them. They shake hands.

Eddy, quickly surveying the front group, offers his assessment: "Looks like you're havin' it rough."

"We have that!" says George Donner. "Indians ran off *eighteen* of our oxen the other night. We also lost our milch cow. Had to yoke up some of the cattle. What about you?"

"No better," answers Eddy. "Hardcoop was lost, and I'm sure is dead. Last night Graves had his horses and one of his cows run off. Had to leave one of his wagons along with Mr. Reed's. Nothin' left to pull it."

"Lost my best mare, and Eddy lost one of his oxen to the Indians," adds Breen. "They shot arrows into a bunch of the cattle. Didn't kill any."

Eddy shakes his head and looks back at the wagons. "Things look awful dark, Mr. Donner."

"For everyone's safety I think we best stay together from this point on," says George Donner.

"You see Reed?" asks Eddy.

"Stayed with us one night," answers George Donner. "Explained what happened. Left the next morning. His man Herron went with him. Had to go on foot cause there weren't no horses for 'im. Won't matter much. The horse Reed was on won't last long. They'll both be on foot soon."

"His wife'll be happy to hear he's safe," says Eddy.

"Said he'd try to get help back to us. I don't know..."

"What's ahead?" asks Breen.

"California?" questions Eddy.

"No way to know how far it is."

It is just before dawn of the next day. One wagon slowly pulls away, creating an opening in the circle that has contained the cattle overnight. Billy Graves and Pike, both on horseback, direct the cattle through the opening and toward a grassy bank farther down the river about a hundred yards away from the encampment.

Later, the two men sit on their horses next to one another watching the cattle graze. Billy yawns and closes his eyes.

"Go on back and get some breakfast, Billy. I'll watch 'em," says Pike.

"All right. I won't be long."

Billy turns his horse and rides in the direction of the camp. Pike watches him go. As Billy reaches camp, the sound of whizzing arrows and painful cries from several of the cattle break the silence.

Pike's head snaps around in time to see that there are a dozen cattle with arrows sticking in them. Some have fallen to their knees; the rest are terrified and look for somewhere to run.

Pike pulls out his double-barreled pistol and looks for the assailants. At first there is no one, then an Indian steps out from behind a bush near the water and lets an arrow go in Pike's direction. Simultaneously, Pike fires and ducks. The arrow passes harmlessly over his head. When he looks again, the Indian has disappeared.

Now, Indians seem to be everywhere, surrounding the location of the cattle. They shoot their arrows at the cattle as fast as possible.

Pike fires again. This time an Indian drops. He reaches for a second pistol and quickly fires two more shots at the closest targets he can find.

His horse, also panicked, rears once and then runs in the direction of the camp. Thirty yards out, Pike manages to swing off the frightened animal. Now he has a double-barreled shotgun in hand.

He drops to one knee, takes careful aim and fires. A second later, he fires again.

In the distance, five men from the camp run toward him.

An hour later, all the men and a few of the women stand looking at the dead and dying cattle, some twenty-one in all. There is nothing

59

they can do but cut off the choicest portions of the meat. The rest would have to be left for the Indians.

After their night of terror the emigrants take stock of what they have left.

The Eddy plight is the worst of all. He has only one ox. Their family is left with no transportation of any kind. About all they can take are the clothes on their back. Even his gun has to be left because it is broken. Rock bottom has arrived.

"What are we to do?" asks Eleanor.

"Put together what little we have and get movin'," answers Eddy.

"What about the children?"

"We'll just have to carry 'em."

"My God! The wagon?"

"Nothin' to do but leave it. Breen's takin' a few of our things in his. Wolfinger's leavin' his. Reinhardt n Spitzer are helping him cache his goods right now. Indians'll most likely take whatever's left anyway."

"What about Margaret and the children?"

"The Donners took 'em in."

"Can we make it?"

"Ain't gonna' lie to you, Ellie. Some say this last stretch is the worst of all."

"Before we get to the Truckee?"

"Yes."

"What about food?"

Eddy climbs up and disappears into their wagon. When he returns he holds up a small package. "We got some sugar. I'll carry that. My gun's busted, but I'll take all the ammunition I have. Maybe I can borrow a gun from someone."

With no other member of the Donner Party in sight, Eddy and his wife struggle forward on foot. Hour after hour passes with Eleanor carrying the baby and William carrying the boy.

Finally the horizon begins to lighten. The Eddys stagger to a spot where three wagons have made a halt. A geyser spring of hot water bubbles to the surface next to the wagons. Eleanor sags to her knees. William sets the boy next to her. Both children appear near death.

William goes to the first wagon and bangs on the rear gate. Tamsen Donner's head appears.

"William!"

"Mrs. Donner, can you help us?"

"We can spare a little coffee. Would that help?"

"God bless you!"

Minutes later, with his hand William scoops some of the boiling hot water from the spring into a cup in which there is a little coffee. He stirs it with a finger and blows on it before he hands it to his wife.

Eleanor tries to revive her daughter by shaking her, but the baby's eyes remain closed. She pries open the child's mouth and carefully pours a little of the liquid into it.

Two hours later the Eddy family are asleep, huddled together under a single blanket. William stirs as one of the wagons, a short distance away, begins to move. He rolls out from under the blanket and gets to his feet. The next wagon begins to roll as well, and the third makes ready to fall in line. Eddy kneels down and gently places his hand on his wife's shoulder. "Ellie … we gotta' get goin'."

Her eyes slowly open, but it is several seconds before she is able to regain her senses. "I can't. I'm so tired."

"I know, but we have to stay close to the wagons."

He lifts her to her feet, and they pick up the children, both of whom appear lifeless.

It is now afternoon of the same day. The forced march continues. Eleanor, concerned, stops to look closely at the baby's face. She shakes her. No response. "Bill, look at Margaret!"

They both drop to their knees. Eddy sets the boy next to him as he takes his daughter into his arms. "They got to have some water!"

He hands the baby back to Eleanor and picks up James. "Follow me, Ellie." They struggle off in the direction of the wagons as fast as they can. Eddy sees Breen walking alongside the wagon as it slowly moves forward.

"Patrick! Stop! I need some water."

"Can't spare it. I need all we have for my family."

"My children will die without it!"

"I got to look out for my own."

"You son-of-a-bitch!"

Eddy goes to the water barrel attached to the side of the wagon and tears the cup from the string. He opens the top.

"God damn you!" yells Breen. "Stay away from that!"

Eddy pulls his knife and turns to face Breen. "I helped you fill this cask! Try 'n stop me and I'll leave you dead right here."

Eleanor arrives. Eddy dips the cup inside. First he pours half into Margaret's mouth and then the rest into James'. He again dips the cup into the barrel and repeats the process. Both children stir and open their eyes. Once again, Eddy fills the cup, this time handing it to his wife. With a menacing look, he turns and faces Breen as he orders his wife to drink.

It is dawn of the next day. The Eddys stagger toward the top of a sandy rise. They both see the lush green grass of a river bottom about two-hundred yards away with aspen and cottonwood trees enclosing it. A broad, swift running Sierra river!

The abandoned wagons rest next to the bank as the Breens, the Murphy clan, and the Graves' family members stand, kneel, or sit in the running water next to the scraggly livestock.

An hour later, as James splashes about in the shallows, William, Eleanor, and the baby sit on the bank with their bare feet in the water.

William takes Eleanor's hand. "Ellie ... there's something I need to say."

"What is it?"

"I'm so sorry. It's my selfishness that's caused this suffering for you and the children."

"Selfishness?"

"It was my dream. An adventure ... a new life. You left your home – your family. I was selfish."

"Sweetheart, I understand why you did it. It was for all of us. It's been a bit rough, but we're almost there."

William looks toward the west. "I hope so."

Later in the day Eddy approaches Breen, sitting next to his wagon.

"Patrick, I need to talk to you."

"Sure."

"Sorry for my behavior earlier."

"Don't give it another thought, William. Is your family all right?"

"Yes, thanks. I do have a favor to ask. I need the loan of your gun. I've seen lots of geese. I think I can provide some meat. We haven't had a thing to eat for more than two days."

"I'll get it for you."

A few hours later, with the midday sun high above, Eddy approaches the encampment with a huge smile on his face. Hanging over his shoulder are nine fat geese!

5

ON TO CALIFORNIA

The party re-forms and the march continues. The number of wagons, however, has shrunk to thirteen. Though they follow the Truckee River, the bottomland disappears. In its place a narrow canyon winds between high, rocky, mountains. Most of the emigrants walk beside their wagons.

On October nineteenth three riders, leading seven pack mules, approach the lead wagon from the west. Though dressed in shirts and trousers, two are clearly Indians, but ... the third? *Stanton!* As he draws close he waves. George and Jacob Donner move out to greet them.

As they unload the pack mules the questions pour forth.

"Where's McCutcheon?" asks George Donner.

"Still at Sutter's," replies Stanton. "Made it through, but was too sick to leave with me. Mr. Sutter was more than generous. Gave us all you see with the offer of more. Even sent along two of his men, Luis and Salvador. They only speak Spanish, so we ain't had much conversation along the way. Good, decent men though, and completely trustworthy. How have you gotten along?"

"Poorly. Lost some good men. Just yesterday an accident took the life of Billy Pike. Wolfinger was killed by Indians. Snyder, Halloran, Hardcoop ... all dead. If you hadn't found us, might be a lot worse."

"Where's Mrs. Reed?"

"In our wagon," answers George Donner. "She's not well. Any news of her husband?"

"I seen him. Four days ago. Hardly recognized 'im. He was barely alive. It was in Bear Valley – just over the pass. Sick as he was he made me promise to take care of his family. Intend to keep that promise."

October 20 –

Mother – I've not written anything for some time. We somehow managed to survive the hardest time you could ever imagine. We lost everything - everything we so carefully packed. All the special treasures you gave me from home. All had to be left behind. I folded what I've written and put it in my pocket. The paper I'm writing this on is borrowed from Mrs. Reed. I don't know when I can get it to someone to take to you and I don't know if I can continue with my promise to record our journey. But please know that I think of you all the time and you are in my prayers every night. All is not bad. Things are much improved since one of the men we sent out has returned with supplies and we are close to California. Still some rough going we understand but we have made it so far. The children have been darlings and my husband is the finest man one could ever know...

The camp is set in the broad Truckee Meadows. It is the twenty-second of October. There is plentiful grass, fresh water, and warm sunshine. Children play. Women work in small groups. A paradise compared to what the company has been through.

Six men (Stanton, Eddy, Breen, Keseberg, George and Jacob Donner) smoke their pipes and drink coffee.

"...but Mr. Sutter said the snows never come before mid-November," says Stanton.

Breen is quick to weigh in. "I don't care what the rest of you decide, I want to get across the pass as soon as possible."

"You're all free to go any time you want," says Geoge Donner. "Our animals need more rest. Jacob and I'll bring up the rear."

"Ellie 'n I talked it over, and we'd like to get started as soon as possible," explains Eddy. "We'll leave when you do, Patrick."

"Fine," says Breen, "Dolan 'n the Kesebergs will too."

"Milt 'n I will look after Mrs. Reed 'n her children," explains Stanton. They need another day's rest before we start."

"Any trouble followin' the trail from here to the pass?" asks Eddy.

"Trail's well marked. Got about fifty miles before you reach Truckee Lake. Should make it in a week if the weather holds. It ain't easy goin', but you seen worse. The pass'll be the problem."

On the trail to the pass the forward party sloshes along through rain and sleet on pine-covered hills. The forward party consists of the wagon-less Eddys and their two children, the Breens and their seven children, the Kesebergs and their two children, Patrick Dolan, and Karl Burger, a teamster for Keseberg. There are several cattle, four horses, and ten oxen. Three of the five wagons belong to Breen, one to Keseberg, and one to Dolan.

Around a blazing fire most of the group are gathered. Snow is falling. In the distance is a solid mass of snow on the high mountains that lie dead ahead.

By the time dawn breaks it is very cold and it is raining, even though there is a foot of snow on the ground. The clouds obscure the mountains ahead. The party, with a sense of urgency, is content with coffee alone before they begin their trek.

6

AT THE LAKE

The forward party arrives at Truckee Lake by mid-day and finds a deserted cabin of saplings and pine branches. Breen and Eddy walk to it and inspect the inside before moving on. The group makes its way alongside the lake moving west. While they fight slushy, wet snow next to the lake, the towering snow-covered peak looms before them.

By the time they reach the base of the mountain at the end of the lake the snow has become at least five feet deep and it is still snowing. The looks on the faces of the pioneers reveal their defeat. Without a word, they turn around and head back in the other direction.

Back at the cabin the Breen family immediately begin to take possession of the cabin. The others take refuge in the wagons. Just before dark the second section, consisting of four wagons and thirty-five emigrants, arrive at the site of the cabin. A fire is built and a brief meal is eaten before everyone seeks shelter from the falling snow.

By mid-morning of the next day, members of the first section, along with a few others from the second, have reached the end of the lake. Even though the weather is decent at this moment, the snow at the level of the lake has reached at least three feet. After only a short distance in their journey up the slopes, all the animals flounder in the snow. It is clear to all that it is hopeless to try to continue with the wagons. Stanton, Eddy, Breen, and Keseberg, all on horseback, have come together.

"We've got to leave the wagons," says Eddy.

"An easy choice for you," answers Breen. "You have none."

"He's right, Patrick. We'll be lucky to get over the pass even without the wagons," explains Stanton.

"Can you find the trail with all this snow?" asks Eddy.

Stanton studies the mountain before he responds. "We'll go first and mark the way as we go. You'd best get your goods packed on the animals as quickly as you can. Time is important."

Three hours later the animals are packed. The mules and horses behave, but the cattle and the oxen, even though exhausted and malnourished, do all they can to shake the packs from their backs. Keseberg, his right foot bandaged, sits on his horse supervising the activities.

"Hurry up, men," yells Keseberg, "we're wasting time."

Breen, losing his patience, replies, "You could get off my damned horse and help us!"

"You know I can't with my foot."

"Then shut up!"

Leading a mule, Stanton, Luis, and Salvador approach the group. Walking along side them is young Virginia Reed. Stanton shouts loud enough for everyone to hear, "We gotta' get movin'! Miss Virginia's mule will be our trailbreaker. We'll drive the animals behind. Everybody keep up!"

The ascent begins. The light rain has turned to snow. The mule, with Virginia holding on, leads the way. Stanton and the two Indians drive the livestock behind. Almost every adult carries a child or anything that might not have found a place in the packs.

Even with the snow beaten down ahead of them, each step requires a major expenditure of energy.

After two hours they have traveled less than two miles. The lead mule is exhausted and mired deep in show. Even so, Stanton's bunch is ahead of the rest. He stops and looks around before he speaks to Virginia.

"We're off the trail. No tellin' where it is. Luis and I are goin' ahead to see if we can find it. Salvador will stay with you."

Back down the mountain the emigrants, near defeat, have stopped to rest. Milt Elliott spots a dead pine tree full of pitch and sets fire to it. It immediately burst into flame. Everyone moves toward it.

Quickly, the rest stop becomes a minor encampment as children are wrapped in blankets and food is taken from the packs.

Meanwhile, further up the mountain Stanton and Luis have reached the summit. The trail is marked! They turn to look back. From their point of view there is no sign of the party except for a line of smoke wafting upward a good distance below them.

On the other side of the pass, facing a strong wind and a very heavy snowfall, Reed and McCutchen work with shovels attempting to free a horse deeply engulfed in snow. Only the horse's nose is visible.

Some twenty yards behind them, two Indian vaqueros with a pack train of about twenty horses struggle along in the trail made by the two men who preceded them.

The lead horse, momentarily freed, is urged on by the two men. It makes a giant leap forward, only to become completely buried again. And again, the two men do their best to free it, but now it becomes obvious to both that their efforts are futile.

McCutchen, speaking loudly to be heard above the fierce wind, admits defeat. "It's no good, Jim. We can't get through this."

"What do we do?" asks Reed. "Go ahead on foot?"

"What good would that do? They need supplies."

"We can't just give up!"

"Even if we could get through – and it don't seem likely – we'd just be two more mouths to feed. We gotta' turn back and try again later."

Back at the site of the emigrants struggle, it is twilight. Stanton, Luis, Salvador, and Virginia enter the "camp." By this time everyone has had something to eat and is making ready to spend the night. The tree has nearly burned itself out, but more wood has been piled against it to keep the fire going.

Stanton looks around, dumbfounded. "What are you doing? Why have you stopped?"

Breen answers: "Look at the women and children! They have to have some rest."

"We made it to the top! You can't stop now. If it snows tonight, we may never make it."

Eddy agrees. "He's right. One more push. We've handled worse than this. What do you say, Patrick?"

"I'll give it a go." volunteers Dolan.

Encouraged by the response, Stanton yells to all, "There you are. On your feet everybody!"

"My foot's killing me," says Keseberg. "I ain't goin' nowhere."

Breen agrees. "That goes for the rest of us. Look around. These people can't make it."

Stanton looks at the sky, shakes his head, and walks to the fire.

During the night an eerie and silent but heavy snowfall continues unabated. By dawn a solid blanket of snow lies over everything. The drifts have risen to more than ten feet.

Suddenly, Keseberg's head appears from beneath the foot of new snow. He looks around and then shouts, "Hello!"

In a semi-circular pattern outward from the tree that provided them warmth the night before, heads and torsos begin to appear out of the snow. Everyone quietly begins to crawl out from under their blankets or hides and gather their belongings for the return trip. In the background the massive snow-covered mountain stands unconquered.

November 6 - I think

I can't remember when I last made an effort to send my thoughts to you. We reached Truckee Lake around the end of October. We have been traveling through snow for days but nothing like it is now. Two attempts to get over the pass have been made. Yesterday our whole bunch gave up halfway up the mountain and made camp right where we quit. In the morning everyone was buried in snow. We made it back to where we set up our meager camp. The children seem fine – tired like all of us. William has become silent. I know he is worried. I try to be of some comfort but with little success. Paper is scarce so I'll end now. God bless you and Father...

November 8 –

It has not stopped snowing for two days. We have seven families in our camp by the lake. The Breens have claimed the cabin that was here. Keseberg built a kind of lean-to next to it. We are with the Murphy bunch a little ways upstream. William found a huge bolder and he and Foster built a cabin using it as one side. Down-stream the Graves clan built a cabin and have taken in the Reed family. Mrs. McCutchen and her baby are also with them. William has counted the members of our camp. There are sixty. Nineteen are men, twelve are women and twenty-nine are children. Our cabins if you could call them that are very crude. They were built quickly and are really nothing more than poles stuck in the ground. We have piled tents and hides and whatever we have on top. It keeps out the snow pretty well, but not the cold. The men have slaughtered some of the oxen and cattle so we do have something to eat. The rest of our party has not made it to the lake. Someone said they stopped a few miles back along a little creek and were camped there. William is going to walk back and see if they are all right. Mrs. Murphy was kind enough to give me some paper so I will write again soon...

It is the tenth of November. Though the sun has broken through for the moment, it is very cold and a light snow is falling. Eddy approaches three crude structures situated near a small creek. The first consists of a tent facing east next to a large pine tree. On the other side, and using the tree as a wall, is a semi-circular lean-to made of pine branches against which hides and odds-and-ends of cloth are placed. Across the stream, and resembling an Indian wigwam, is the third hovel. Smoke rises from the center of each.

Eddy studies each for several seconds before, he calls out. "Hello!"

A moment later, George Donner appears at the opening of the first "cabin." His hand is bandaged.

"William! Are you alone?"

"Yes. I've been out hunting. We were worried. Thought I'd see if I could find you. Saw your fire. Is everyone all right?"

"Tolerable. We stopped here when the goin' got too hard. My family and Mrs. Wolfinger is in here. That's Jacob's there, and our teamsters are across the creek. Would you like a cup of coffee?"

"I sure would. Thanks."

Donner goes inside the tent and reappears a few seconds later. He hands a cup to Eddy. "What news have you?"

"Nothin' good. We're camped near Truckee Lake. There was an old cabin there already. The Breens took it, 'n Keeseberg put up a lean-to next to it. Us and the Murphys put up a cabin upstream from theirs. There's one more downstream – a double one. The Graves is in one part 'n the Reeds 'n their people in the other half. Took a count a couple 'a days ago. There are sixty of us."

"What about food?"

"Most have started slaughtering the livestock they have. I've hunted every day. Best I could do was a coyote and two ducks."

"What about the pass?"

"Made a try at it. Stanton even got over, but it was too tough goin'
for the rest. There's talk of another try when the weather calms down.
How'd you hurt your hand?"

"Cut it with a chisel. It's nothin'."

November 8 –

*William found the Donners and their group. There were 21
of them. They have six men, three women, and twelve
children. Added to our sixty it means that we are down to
eighty-one who have made it this far. There is talk of
another attempt but the weather is still awful...*

November 10 –

*The supplies brought by Mr. Stanton are now gone. Most
of the animals have been slaughtered. Some of our people
are much better off than others. I'm sorry to say that a
good many of our fellow travelers are concerned only for
themselves. They have turned away from others in our
group who were far less fortunate than they were. Mrs.
Reed and the eight people she is responsible for are facing
starvation because they have almost nothing left to them.
William has gone out hunting every day but has found
almost no game. He shot two ducks yesterday, but had to
give one away for the loan of the gun. Mr. Graves had an
ox that had starved to death but rather than give it away,
we were forced to buy it from him because we have little
else...*

It was decided that another attempt at the pass was all that was left
to the party. On the twelfth of November, a group of fifteen made ready
for the attempt. Thirteen of the strongest men and two of the young
women, Mrs. Fosdick and her sister, Mary Graves, gathered at dawn to
begin their effort. By nightfall they were back completely defeated. The

75

snow was still as deep, if not deeper, and was still too soft to support the weight of a person.

With no other source of food available, Eddy still continued to hunt each day though he had encountered almost no wildlife. This morning it would appear his luck has changed. He can see tracks in the snow. On close examination he becomes aware that they are tracks of a grizzly. A grizzly! His only weapon is a single shot muzzle-loader. Against a grizzly?

He studies the weapon in his hand for several seconds, looks at the tracks again, and makes his decision. He will follow the trail.

Minutes later, about seventy-five yards away, he can see a monstrous grizzly digging roots. Eddy quickly ducks down and crawls on all fours toward a large pine tree. Once there he reaches into his pocket and pulls out his one remaining bullet and places the ball in his mouth. He uncorks his power horn and brings it to a ready position.

After a deep breath he raises the gun and settles on his target – the upper portion of the bear's back. He carefully steadies his weapon. He slowly squeezes the trigger. The sound of the powder exploding precedes ever so slightly the frightening roar of the wounded beast.

Quickly it rises on its hind legs and turns to find its attacker. The lingering gun smoke provides the information it seeks. Immediately it bolts toward Eddy on all fours, its mouth open wide with a roar of rage.

In a shockingly short time the animal closes the distance between the two. Eddy, fighting to control his fear, manages to pour the powder. By this time the bear is upon him. All Eddy can manage to do is duck behind the tree as a giant paw swipes at him when the bear crashes past him.

Eddy slams home the ball and steps around the tree to fire again. The bear is on its back, but it quickly rights itself and again charges.

This time Eddy adroitly scoots around the tree as the bear passes. He directs his second shot at the gigantic back. A second hit!

The bear continues to roar loudly as it lies thrashing on the ground. With blood bubbling from the two wounds and from its mouth, the grizzly glares at the man.

Eddy, now ready to run in any direction, watches the animal continue to rage in pain. He looks around for any kind of weapon and finds a large branch lying only a few feet away. He grabs it and begins his own attack.

He brings the club crashing down across the bear's face. Again! And again! And again! He continues the bashing even after the bear has clearly lost consciousness.

Finally, completely exhausted, he falls backward to the ground to survey his vanquished foe.

A short while later Eddy approaches the camp. He shouts as loudly as is possible: "Hey! Hey everybody! I got a grizzly!" Patrick appears at the opening to his cabin. "Patrick! I killed a grizzly! Two shots! I need the loan of a yoke of oxen to bring it in."

"You bet. I'll help you drag it – for a share."

"Sure. We'll have *meat* tonight!"

November 15 –

William killed a bear yesterday! A big grizzly. We had to give half the meat for the loan of the gun. After giving several others a share we got to keep the rest. Doesn't seem quite fair considering the way the others have been acting. But you can't know how wonderful it was to give the children meat again. It means so much to see smiles on the childrens faces. Can't remember how long it has been...

The third week of November had arrived. Each day everyone's spirit declined a little. Most were ailing in some way and few possessed enough energy to manage much more than the daily essentials. And the snow continued to fall. Its level was well above the top of the cabins.

Milt Elliott, wearing a pair of crude snowshoes, heads in the direction of a line of smoke that drifts upward through a hole in the snow. He arrives at a depression in the snow and disappears into the hole below.

He descends into what looks like a storm cellar below white ground – a "double cabin" with a wall of pine branches dividing it into two parts. A number of crude beds made from the wooden planks taken from the wagons are spread around the dirt floor. At the far end is a hearth made from piled rocks.

Spread about the eastern half of the hovel are eleven people: Margaret Reed and her four children, Stanton, Luis, Salvador, James Smith, Baylis Williams, and his sister, Eliza. Elliott drops the wood he was carrying next to the hearth and then goes to where Stanton is making snowshoes. U-shaped oxen yokes have been sawed into strips to make them lighter and more manageable.

Elliott joins Margaret Reed as she watches Stanton thread strips of rawhide back and forth through holes in the wood. A stack of already completed shoes is piled next to his cot.

"How's the shoes work?" asks Stanton.

"Not bad," replies Elliott, "a little hard to get used to, but they work. How's Baylis?"

Margaret answers. "Getting weaker all the time. Do you still plan to try to make it to the Donners today?"

"Yes, ma'am. Just wanted to get a little wood for you all before I left. Eddy's goin' with me."

"Won't be gone long will you?" asks Stanton.

"Should take two or three hours to get there. Find out if anyone wants to join us, borrow a compass, and that's it."

"They'll want to hear our news," says Margaret. "You'd best stay the night."

"Do we have enough shoes?" asks Elliott.

"I think so," says Stanton. " Don't know for sure how many's goin'. What's the weather like?"

"It was nice earlier, but it ain't lookin' so good now. Well, best be goin'. I'll say hello for you, Mrs. Reed."

"Thank you, Milt."

Hours later, Elliott and Eddy are in the middle of a serious snowstorm. They plod along, looking around as they go. Elliott points to some smoke spreading upward from the snow. They quickly find the opening to the cabin. Elliott shouts, "Hello! Mr. Donner!"

A flap of canvas is lifted and Tamsen Donner's head appears. "Who is it?"

"Milt Elliott and William Eddy, Mrs. Donner."

"Hurry inside, men."

To prevent the snow piled on top of the canvas from entering, they carefully pull back the flap just enough to make room for their entrance.

Inside, everyone remains lying in bed, but smile and nod. George Donner is propped up on one elbow. His left hand is still heavily bandaged. He extends his other hand to the men. "Hello, William ... Milt. Good to see you."

They shake hands, then the two go the fire to warm themselves.

"How are you, Mr. Donner?" asks Eddy.

"A little better today. Got some sun yesterday. Got outta' this damned hole and moved around a bit. My hand has been hurting somethin' awful."

"It's infected," says Tamsen.

"See you're wearing snowshoes," observes Donner.

"Yes, sir," answers Elliott. "Stanton and Mr. Graves made 'em outta' oxen yokes."

"Any word of Reed?"

"None," says Elliott.

"Sure thought he'd have been here by now."

"If it was humanly possible he would have," says Eddy.

"Any more attempts at the pass?"

"Let's see … two since we last talked to you," answers Elliott. "The first one didn't get nowhere. On the second, Eddy 'n a couple 'a others got across, but came back for the rest. Stanton's mules couldn't make it. He 'n the Indians wouldn't leave 'em. Thought Sutter would be mad."

"How long ago was that?"

"Better 'n two weeks."

"Weather's been awful ever since," explains Eddy. "No let up. But they's ready to try again. That's why we're here – to see if anyone wants to try it."

"Jacob's folks are no better off than we are. And we haven't even seen our men for about a week. Be obliged if you'd check on them."

"Sure will," says Eddy.

"How your people holdin' up?" asks Donner.

Eddy answers, " Poorly. That's why we gotta' have another go at it."

"Food's run out," adds Elliott. "Folks are boilin' animal hides."

"What animals we did have run off durin' the last storm. Ain't nobody found 'em," says Eddy.

"Who's goin,?" asks Donner.

"Last count, 'bout fifteen. Breen's sick. Keseberg's foot's worse. Spitzer's too weak, and Balis Williams is about dead."

Donner shakes his head. "Sure don't know what will become 'a all 'a us if someone don't make it."

"God knows that's true!" agrees Elliott.

"Could you use some tobacco, men?" asks Donner.

"Yes, sir. Thank you."

"After you check on the men, you're welcome to sleep here. The floor's all we got."

An hour later, outside, Elliott and Eddy stand looking in the direction of the men's cabin. Smoke may be seen rising from Jacob Donner's location, but nothing from the teamsters.

Confused, the men walk in the general direction of its location, looking around as they go. Eddy stops and points at a mound between two trees. Elliott nods and they move toward it. Once there they drop to their knees in a low spot and begin to poke around. Both shout: "Hello!"

From within, a weak voice replies, "Hello."

The two men now begin to dig the snow back with their hands. Finally, they reach the frozen flap and lift it. Both recoil from the stench of air that strikes them. It takes a second for them to recover before they enter.

Inside, the conditions are worse than horrible. There is filth everywhere. Vomit and excrement cover the small floor. The four men lie in their beds with everything they can find piled on for warmth. Snow covers what was once their fireplace. The only one who appears to be conscious is John Denton, and he barely has the strength to follow the movements of the two men.

In a barely audible voice, Denton mumbles, "Thank God. I thought we were dead."

Eddy, holding his hand over his face, asks, "How long have you been like this?"

Though labored, Denton is able to reply. "No idea. Can't remember when I last had anything to eat."

Elliott turns and moves toward the door. "I'll get a fire goin'. We'll ask the Donners for some food."

Minutes later Elliott has gathered some wood and starts a fire. Immediately, smoke fills the room. He grabs a pole and pokes upward above the fire. Once the hole is formed in the snow, the smoke is drawn toward it.

A minute later the flap opens and Eddy enters. He carries a piece of meat about the size of his hand.

"Said it was all she could spare," explains Eddy.

"Jesus! I'll get some water boilin'. Some broth's better 'n nothin'

7

A FINAL ATTEMPT

Under one blanket William and Eleanor Eddy lie on the floor of the cabin. The children lie between them.

"William, will you make me a promise?"

"Anything, sweetheart."

"Promise me you'll do what's right. Your worry about us is keeping you from it." William does not respond. Eleanor continues. "You can make it."

"I can't leave you this way."

"You must. It's our only chance to survive."

"But you –"

"The children would never make it. My place is here with them. You're our only hope. You must go."

William starts to speak but Eleanor gently places her hand on his lips.

It is a clear day. Eddy, Stanton, and Dolan stand outside the cabin looking at the snow-covered pass with the sun shining on it.

Eddy speaks first. "God, I was wonderin' if we'd every see the sun again."

"We gotta' take advantage of this break. Go as soon as we can."

"How many snowshoes we got?" asks Eddy.

"Fourteen pair, not countin' Milt's and Noah's."

"Why ain't they back?" asks Dolan.

"Cause 'a the blizzard I'm sure."

"Should we wait for 'em? Make another trip to the Donners?"

"Best to conserve our energy," answers Stanton. "They may be here before we go. Gonna' take a little time to get ready."

"How long?" ask Dolan.

"Maybe day after tomorrow – first light."

"We sure who's goin'?"

"Seventeen by my count," says Stanton.

Eddy uses his fingers to count. "Us three. Luis, Salvador, Uncle Billy. That's six."

Stanton continues the count. "The Fosters. Jay Fosdick 'n his wife. Mary. Harriet Pike. Antonio. Burger."

"That's fourteen," says Eddy.

"There's Mrs. McCutchen," adds Stanton.

"What about her baby?"

"Leavin' it with Mrs. Graves." After the others look doubtful, Stanton explains. "Got her mind set on it. So's Mrs. Murphy about her two boys goin'."

"That makes seventeen," says Eddy. "You said fourteen pair of shoes. That's three short."

"The two boys can bring up the rear. Use the tracks of the others. Burger volunteered to do the same."

"Think they can do it?" asks Eddy.

"I don't know. Didn't figure it was up to me to decide. Anyone's got the right to give it a try."

"That's five women," says Dolan.

"Hell, they's holdin' up better 'n the men. And this time we gotta' travel light. Figure we need to make at least five miles a day."

"How many days will it take?" asks Dolan.

"Five might get us far enough to find help."

"We planned enough rations for six," says Eddy. "That's not much. Hell, we ain't got much."

"We gotta' take a rifle for any game we see. A few pistols. A hatchet for firewood. Some coffee."

Eddy adds to the planning. "Not even a change 'a clothes. A blanket ... 'n that's about it. Mary Graves has even given our bunch a name – Forlorn Hope."

"Sure hope the weather holds."

"It's gotta'."

Day 1

About twenty people are gathered in front of the Breen cabin. From the Graves/Reed cabin a small group emerges. The first two are Eddy and Dolan. They carry something that is wrapped in a blanket. Following them are two women.

The group moves to a spot in the clearing. Once there, the two men gently lower their burden into a hole in the snow. They step back and move to the other side of the two women. After several seconds the two women turn and trudge toward their cabin. After they leave, the men begin to shovel snow into the hole over the body of Baylis Williams.

An hour later in front of the Breen cabin the group makes preparations to leave. The trekkers do their best to accustom themselves to the awkward snowshoes. Most wobble around, testing their stability. One, having fallen, remains seated on the snow. Some merely stand still, conserving energy. Most of the onlookers are amused by their clumsy antics.

As Eddy and Dolan approach the group, the activity ceases and the mood of excitement subsides.

"How's Eliza holdin' up?" asks Breen about the condition of Williams' sister.

"Well as could be expected," answers Eddy.

"When did he die?"

"Middle of the night sometime."

"Ladies'll be goin' over later," says Breen. "S'pose she'd like to be alone for a while."

"I 'spose. Mrs. Reed's with her."

Stanton speaks to the group. "Folks, we're losin' valuable time. Better say your goodbyes."

Two hours later the journey is underway. Eddy is the leader, with Stanton directly behind him. Following them are Mary Graves, Amanda McCutchen, Franklin Graves, Jay Fosdick, and his wife Sarah. Next are Luis, Salvador, and Antonio. Finally, Dolan, followed by Bill Foster.

The two Murphy boys, Lem and William, assisted by Karl Burger, bring up the rear. Without the snowshoes, the going for these three is much worse than anticipated. With each step they sink nearly to their waist. For the boys it is exhausting work. Their sisters, Sarah Foster and Harriet Pike have dropped back to help them along.

By afternoon, under clear skies, the line is now well spread out. For the boys at the end, it is torture. Lem courageously struggles on, but William is barely able to move forward without someone's help. He is crying and begging to stop. The sisters do all they can, but it is not enough.

Burger, half carrying the boy, finally gives in to his frustrations and stops. The boy immediately slumps to the snow, sobbing.

"No good!" announces Burger. "The boy goes back."

"We can't give up so soon," pleads Harriet.

"He cannot make it. You go on. I take him back. No shoes – no chance."

Lem bravely holds his ground. "I'm not going back. I can make it."

86

"Not talking 'bout you. This boy and I go now."

Burger grabs the boy's hand and turns toward the cabins, almost dragging the crying boy as he goes.

"Stop crying and stand up!" commands Burger roughly. He looks at the rest. "Good luck!"

Speechless, the sisters watch them go.

By nightfall the group has only reached the end of the lake. The men take turns using their only hatchet to chop the trees that are being used as the platform on which they will build the fire. The sisters, with Lem between them, approach.

"Mr. Stanton, Lem must have some snowshoes," says Sarah.

"What do I use to make them?" asks Stanton.

"We have to think of something," adds Harriet.

"See those mounds of snow over there?" says Eddy. "Underneath are the wagons we abandoned on our first try. Maybe you can find something in them."

Without a word, Harriet and Sarah move toward the mounds.

Later, everyone except Stanton who is busy creating a pair of snowshoes from an old pack-saddle, huddle close together next to the platform of "green" logs on which a fire burns brightly.

December 17 –

Yesterday I faced the worst moment of my life. I watched my dear husband leave us and I know I may never see him again. We both realize that if he and those with him do not make it across the pass and return soon our childrens lives are over. My appeal to him to leave was successful only because of them. I try to remain strong for their sake but I know I am weak. I think often of closing my eyes and not waking and it takes all my will to - Forgive me mother for pouring out my heart this way. I'm sure you will never see the words I write but it is a comfort to reach out and feel that I am with you ...

Day 2

It is early morning. The group's movement is now up the side of the mountain. Each grim-faced member sloshes forward.

By nightfall Stanton and Eddy pull themselves up on a huge boulder, free of snow. Minutes later, the last person is helped up by Eddy.

"Look around, folks," says Eddy. "This is the top!" At the end of the lake below, a thin line of smoke rises from each of the cabins. "Don't look so far away do they? Tomorrow we got to make up a little time."

Day 3

In bright sunshine the line winds its way downhill. The great, white expanse of a valley lies before them.

Stanton's eyes are constantly squinting, a sign of snow-blindness, and a certain lethargy indicates his concession to a combination of fatigue and hunger. He steps to the side of the trail and leans against a tree. Those who pass him hardly notice.

By the evening the foundation has been formed, and the fire roars. Everyone sits close to it, making ready for a night of rest.

Out of the dark, Stanton appears and walks to the fire to warm himself. He is barely alive. All eyes are on him, but no words are directed at him.

December 19 –

William and the rest have been gone for two days. It seems like forever. There is little else to do but tend to the children. Some kind souls bring firewood now and then.

When the fire dies out the cold is unbearable. I do my best
to keep the little ones huddled close to me ...

Day 4

After the march begins, almost nothing is said by anyone. The emigrants can manage little more than lifting one foot at a time to place in the track ahead. The line lengthens as the day wears on requiring Eddy to return several times to spur on the stragglers. Several requests are made to make camp early in order to rest. Finally, Eddy consents and a fire is built.

Day 5

It is a day like the one before. The group now struggles up a small rise. Stanton is at the end of his strength. He drops to his knees and then topples over into a fetal position. He closes his eyes as though preparing for sleep.

A strong hand grabs him by the wrist and pulls his arm upward.

"Mr. Stanton!" growls Mary. "No time to rest. Let's go!"

Stanton looks up with a kindly smile on his face. "Just a few minutes. You go on."

"No! We'll rest a little bit."

Stanton looks up trying to see the person. "Who is it?"

"Mary Graves, Mr. Stanton."

"Mary, I'm blind. No good to anyone. Just let me rest a bit."

Marry forcibly pulls him up, shaking him as she does so. "Get on your feet and get moving!"

"I can't –"

"*Yes* you can! Now *move!*" With her help he follows her command.

Little did they know they were near the site where Reed and McCutchen had turned back weeks ago and only a few miles from where they had placed a cache of food.

Day 6

The group huddles next to the fire. Each member has a small cup of coffee and a small strip of beef. The men smoke their pipes. Wrapped in their blankets, they chew as slowly as possible to forestall the beginning of the day's journey.

Finally, Eddy straps on his snowshoes and gets to his feet. "Best get movin', folks."

The Indians stir themselves and follow his lead. The rest continue their vacant stare.

"Come on," encourages Eddy. "We're losin' time."

Almost in unison, the women respond. They find their snowshoes and begin to strap them on.

Dolan remains unmoved. "How we gonna' make it? There's no end in sight. We ain't gone more'n twenty miles."

Foster agrees. "Ain't no end to the Goddamn snow!"

Dolan continues his argument. "Coffee's gone. One little piece of meat left. What's the use?"

"We just gotta' go on," says Mary. "To give up now means death, and we all know it."

"She's right," says Eddy firmly. "On your feet!"

Slowly they all stir and begin their preparations, except for Stanton.

"Come on, Mr. Stanton," says Mary. "Time to go."

"You go ahead. Just wanna' finish my pipe."

She studies him for several seconds, then slowly turns away to join the others.

Near a canyon wall in the late afternoon, the wind is blowing and it is snowing. The two Indians and Eddy, in the lead, have stopped. To their right, and west, is a canyon wall that appears almost impossible to traverse. To the left, and south, is a downhill slope that seems inviting. Luis and Salvador converse quietly.

Eddy looks to them for an answer. "Which way?" Again, the Indians talk. Finally they point to the ridge. "You sure? Where the hell's Stanton? He'd know." Again the Indians point to the canyon wall.

Eddy shakes his head. "I don't think we can make it. We'd best camp here and wait for the others. Maybe Stanton'll be with 'em." He drops to his knees and pulls off his small pack. The other two men do the same.

As Eddy reaches inside his pack to get the hatchet, he notices a small package about the size of his fist. He takes it out. A note is attached:

My Dearest Husband –

Hurry back to us for we need you so.

Your own dear Eleanor.

He quickly opens the package and, with tears in his eyes, finds a small chunk of the bear meat.

Day 7

Everyone is huddled together close to the fire. Mary is on her feet pouring hot water into everyone's cup.

"Hot water sure don't do much," complains Foster.

"It's something!"

"Which way from here, Mr. Eddy?" asks Amanda.

"I don't know. Hoped Stanton might catch up."

91

"Hell, we ain't gonna' see him no more," says Foster.

"The Indians think we should stay west, but I don't know if we can get over that wall," explains Eddy.

"Looks awful hard to me," says Sarah.

"I think we can make it if we move south a ways. We'll find a way through."

"Those clouds look mighty dark," warns Mary. "Best do somethin'."

An hour later a serious snowstorm is upon them. Strong winds make the going impossible. They take shelter behind an outcropping of rocks. Eddy and the Indians are some distance away from the huddled group cutting wood for the fire.

Day 8

From a mound of snow next to the smoldering platform a small eruption occurs and Eddy's head appears. "Time to get goin'!"

Small tremors appear from below the snow and other heads reach the surface.

An hour later everyone stands looking at a flat spot on the ridge of the canyon, Eddy starts the trek and the others take their places in line.

On the ridge in late afternoon there is snow everywhere, in every direction. It is a terribly frightening sight, particularly with more mountains in the distance. An enormous territory to traverse!

Day 9

In a snow-covered wilderness the crisis of the emigrants' weakened state is now matched by the fury of a major snowstorm. The wind-driven snow makes it difficult to see more than a few feet ahead. Close together now, they make a puny effort at progress.

Finally, the group becomes a solid mass as they seek to combine and retain their warmth.

"We gotta turn back!" yells Foster.

"We can't go back," says Mary. "We gotta' keep movin'." Though the sound of the wind makes it difficult to hear, the other women voice their agreement.

By this time, Dolan is raging. "Lord Jesus showed us the way! Eat my flesh and drink my blood. We must follow his words!"

"Shut up," yells Foster. "You're crazy!"

"Crazy am I? We're all going to starve! Someone must give their body to the rest!"

"Be quiet!"

"Draw lots to see whose flesh must be used to keep the rest alive."

"Fine with me," says Eddy, "but let's do it like a man. Two of us take out our gun and fight to the death."

"Stop that talk!" says Mary. "We're not animals."

Franklin Graves, no longer able to stand, slumps to the snow. Mary and Sarah immediately get him back on his feet.

Eddy takes charge. "We gotta' make camp. Get a fire goin'. Get everyone over by that tree." He grabs the two Indians and they move away from the group.

Later, the three men join the group huddled next to the trunk of a tree. They carry armfuls of green logs. As Luis begins to form the foundation for the fire, the other two stagger away to get the wood for burning.

Still later, the fire is burning briskly. Everyone is gathered about it as closely as is safe.

"The rest 'a you men – get up and get some more wood. We got it goin'." There is no response. "Dolan! Foster! Fosdick! Antonio! Get up!"

Slowly, Foster and Fosdick rise to their feet. Dolan and Antonio, in a trance, remain unmoved. Eddy shakes his head and hands the hatchet to Foster. "Get as much as you can. It's gonna' be a hard night."

Two hours later, exhausted and numb, everyone is huddled next to the fire. Eddy picks up the hatchet and stands. He wraps his blanket securely around himself and heads out into the darkness.

Some distance from the fire, Eddy stops, reaches into his pocket and withdraws his last bite of bear meat. It is barely larger than his thumbnail, but as he places it in his mouth, a look of ecstasy shows on his face.

The cold drives him on to his task. With just enough light from the fire, he finds a dead tree and begins to hack away at the branches.

Back at the fire minutes later, Eddy adds the wood to a small pile a few feet away from the fire. He finds an open spot and lies down, wrapping the blanket around himself as he does so.

Eddy surveys the others around the fire in their tortured sleep. Antonio is clearly in serious trouble. His breathing is labored. His head rolls from side to side, and his upper body is uncovered.

Antonio's arm swings out to the side and his hand comes to rest on some coals at the edge of the fire. No reaction! After a couple of seconds, the hand starts to smoke.

Eddy, shocked by what he is seeing, pulls himself up and reaches across another body to grab the arm to pull the hand away from the fire.

Eddy then resumes his spot next to the fire and watches the misery of the little cattle herder. Antonio continues to writhe, and in a matter of seconds the hand is back in the fire. This time it shrivels in flame.

Eddy slowly closes his eyes. When he opens them a short time later, the hand is nothing more than a red-hot coal. The little Mexican lies quietly.

As the night wears on the intensity of the storm increases. Foster notices that the fire has diminished in warmth. He goes to the pile of

94

wood and tosses all that's left on the fire. Satisfied with the new warmth, he wraps himself in his blanket and takes his place next to it.

A short while later the small foundation logs have not been sufficient to contain the heat. Gaps have formed between them, melting the snow below. As a result, the burning wood and the foundation itself have settled into the hole it created.

Eddy is the first to notice. He quickly gets up, finds the hatchet, and heads out to renew the supply.

Away from the fire, Eddy chops away at a dead branch. As he takes the hatchet back the head flies off well behind him. As his hand moves forward the shocking loss becomes apparent. In terror he hurries back and searches about desperately. Gone forever!

Back at the fire the hole grows ever deeper and wider. Most are now aware that they, along with the fire, are sinking. Where panic should be, simple apathy exists.

An hour later the bottom of the hole is now more than six feet deep and at the level of the ground below. A wall of snow surrounds the people, most of whom are on their feet, standing in slush and water.

Antonio's body lies at the base of the wall. Graves is supported by Mary and Sarah, and Harriet does her best to keep Lem upright. Luis squats next to the wall in a stupor.

Dolan, still wrapped in his blanket, lies partially submerged in the water at the bottom of the hole.

Eddy and Foster work to get the partially burned logs to stand on end, above the water. With this accomplished, they gingerly pick up the still burning pieces of wood and place them on top, safely away from the water below. Though difficult to maintain, it does provide some heat. Everyone who is able helps to keep the fire going.

Suddenly, as though thrust upward by an invisible force, Luis lunges forward into the "fire on stilts" as he emits a scream. The precarious arrangement tumbles to the ground and hisses violently for several seconds.

Eddy screams, "Oh, God, no!" With only the light from a few glowing embers left, Eddy launches into action. He goes to a side of the wall and digs into it, making a path upward. "Listen to me! Grab someone and climb out of here! Do it now!"

Eddy grabs the first person he can get his hands on and shoves that person toward the "stairway." Then he gropes around on the floor until he finds Antonio's body. He rips the blanket free from the body and scrambles out of the hole. Once out, he spreads the blanket out on the surface of the snow and looks around. The first person he sees is Mary.

"Mary!" Get everyone on the blanket!"

Back down in the hole goes Eddy. He gropes around, grabbing anything he can get his hands on. He finds another blanket and drapes it over his shoulder; then he stumbles over someone lying on the ground. He drops down and pulls the person into a sitting position. Dolan! Using all his strength he drags him toward the exit and then up and out.

By this time the group is huddled together on the blanket. All this has become too much for young Samuel. In his exhausted and malnourished state, the trauma of these events has exacted its toll on him. He becomes delirious and tries to escape contact with the huddled mass while Mary does her best to hold him down. Slowly, the boy calms and lapses into unconsciousness. By this time Eddy has carried Dolan to a spot next to the rest. He looks around. "Is this everyone?"

"I think so," answers Mary.

Eddy speaks loudly to the group. "Listen to me! Sit down – put your backs toward the middle. Get as close as you can!"

Most follow his directions. Those who cannot are directed and positioned by the ones who still have their wits about them.

Once they are bunched together, Eddy takes his blanket and the one he found and spreads them over the people. After this he crawls under the blankets and works his way into the huddled mass.

December 24 –

The word is that tomorrow is Christmas. I have lost track of days and time. I did everything I could think of to create some merriment for the children but they did not understand. We tried to sing carols and I told stories but they have little energy because their food is so limited. They spend much of their time sleeping – maybe that is best...

Day 10 – Christmas Day

It is morning and everyone is still under the blankets. It is still snowing. A muffled moaning may be heard from within the mound of snow. It gradually grows in volume until it becomes a crazed scream. The surface of the snow at the edge of the mound ripples and then explodes.

Out from under their "ceiling" for the night, Dolan bursts into the open, flailing his arms and ranting wildly. He flounders in the snow in his attempt to run away. He tears at his clothing and succeeds in removing his coat. Next he rips away at his shirt, quickly reducing it to shreds on the snow.

Eddy appears and makes his way toward Dolan who, in turn, opens his arms as though to welcome him. "William! Let's go! Let's get away from this awful place!"

Eddy picks up Dolan's coat and tries to wrap it around him. Dolan throws it away. "William, this is our chance!"

This time Eddy takes him by the arm and pulls him toward the mound. "Patrick, let's get back inside. We can talk about it there."

Infuriated, Dolan throws Eddy down, turns and begins to claw his way through the snow. "You bastard! I'll go by myself!"

Eddy rises quickly from the snow and makes a grab at him. Dolan turns to face him. "Try and stop me and I'll kill you!"

Eddy gives in to the inevitable. He makes his way back to the mound where he stops to watch Dolan who now fights through the snow, screaming at the top of his lungs as he moves away.

Later in the day still under their "tent" of blankets, muffled moans and the labored breathing of the suffering inhabitants may be heard. Then an anguished wail, followed by gut-wrenching sobs.

Mary, recognizing the sobs to be coming from her sister, calls to her: "Sarah! What is it?"

"It's father!" says Sarah, now hysterical. "He's not breathing! Mary, he's dead!"

Seconds later, the blanket on one side is thrown back and light enters the enclosure. Mary is bent over her dead father. His head is cradled in Sarah's lap. Tears roll down her cheeks.

As the two sobbing daughters focus on their father's lifeless body, Foster reaches outside to grab the blanket. As he does so, he sees Dolan lying only a few feet away. "William! Patrick's out here!"

With considerable pain, Eddy pulls himself to the opening. Dolan's body, nearly naked from the waist up, lies face down in the snow.

"Is he alive?" asks Eddy.

Foster works his way out to him and turns him over. "My God, he's still breathing!"

"Pull him inside."

As Foster does so, he closes the blanket back over them.

Day 11

It has stopped snowing and the sun has broken through. The blanket on one side is slowly lifted and thrown back. Mary crawls outside, looking up at the blue sky. "Dear God, it's over! The sun is shining!"

The blanket is pulled back farther. Eddy and Foster stumble out into the open. The remaining women pull themselves up and join the others outside. In the open now, the two Indians, their blankets wrapped securely about them, remain seated, but look up at the sun above.

"Can we have a fire, Mr. Eddy?"

Eddy reaches in his pocket, pulls out his flint and steel, and then looks around for something to burn. "I need some dry tinder. Anyone have anything dry?"

The rest examine their clothes, searching for anything that is not soaked. Mary removes her mantle and turns it inside out.

"I need your knife," says Mary.

Eddy hands it to her, and she cuts through the lining of the coat. She reaches inside and pulls out some cotton. She feels it, blows on it, and holds it up. "Will this do?"

Eddy takes it and rubs it between his fingers. "I think so. Now we'll need some dry wood."

An hour later a fire reaches up a dead pine tree that towers well above the snow. On pine boughs laid out on the snow, the survivors (five men and five women) sit as close to the fire as possible. They stare dully at the fire in front of them. No display of emotion. No conversation. No movement.

Everyone is now completely exhausted, a result of their struggles through the snow of course, but also because they have not had anything to eat for days. They now know they cannot continue in their current condition, and so it becomes clear that this leaves them to face a moral dilemma: accept death or survive. But survival can mean only one thing – they must use the flesh of their dead comrades to sustain their own lives.

Finally, Foster slowly stands, turns away from the fire, pulls a knife from his belt, and walks away from the group. Every person watches Foster leave. He moves toward the four bodies (Antonio, Graves, Dolan, and Lem) laid out next to one another on the snow. He stands stiffly looking down for several seconds before he drops to his knees. He is next to Dolan's body, which is naked to the waist. The eyes are open as though looking at the sky above.

Foster carefully places the tip of his knife in the center of the stomach. At this instant he becomes aware that the rest are watching him. He pulls himself up and steps over the body. Once again, he drops to his knees. This time his back is to the group, blocking their view.

Later, everyone is squatted next to the fire. On a crude spit leaning against the tree, strips of flesh roast next to the open flames.

Sobbing as they slowly chew, all partake of the human flesh except for the two Indians who remain apart by their own fire, and Eddy, who has completely removed himself from the group. Everyone is most careful to avoid eye contact with one another.

Days 12, 13, 14

The next three days are spent resting and recovering enough strength to move on. They are in horrible condition. Most have suffered frostbite and as their feet dry, they ooze blood, making it painful even to put weight on them. The snowshoes are falling apart and each person does what he or she can to fashion some kind of repair. All the while, of course, they are trying to regain at least a degree of strength from the human flesh that is available. When they do so, each is careful to avoid partaking of the flesh of a relative or loved one.

December –

My Darling Husband –

It has been almost two weeks since you left. I pray each night that you are safe and have made it through. After you left, Milt made it back from the Donners' camp. Jacob is dead. Three of his men as well. Life here has been hard. Our food supply is gone. The best we can do is to boil the hides we have, and there are only a few left. I heard that Mr. Burger died last night, but we almost never see anyone. We spend most of our time in bed wrapped in our blankets. The only time we leave is to get wood for the fire. The poor, starved children are too weak to cry. I don't know how much longer we can last. Your loving children and I miss you terribly. May God watch over you.

We love you.

Eleanor

Day 15

Leaning against a tree, Eddy remains apart from the rest of the survivors who are solemnly removing strips of flesh from drying racks made of pine branches. As they do so they place them in their packs.

As Eddy stares at the mountains in the distance a voice disturbs his reverie: "We're about ready to go," says Mary.

"Oh ... all right."

"William, you must eat something."

"Something! Call it what it is!"

Mary is now crying. "God, I know what we've done. But we're alive."

"I'm alive!"

Mary speaks quietly to herself. "But for how long?"

By dusk the snow has been cleared away from a dead tree and the group sits next to the tree as it burns. Most are eating. Lying on the ground away from the others, Eddy appears to be asleep. Mary kneels beside him.

"William. William! Wake up."

Eddy's eyes open and he offers a friendly smile. "Hello Ellie. Are we home yet?"

"William, you've got to eat! You're dying. Do you understand? You're dying!"

"I am kinda hungry, Ellie."

Mary quickly rises, goes to the fire, picks a strip of the meat from the spit, and returns. "Here you are, William."

Still in a trance, he accepts it and takes a small bite. As he chews he stares into the darkness of the night.

Day 16

The group is on the move. The two Indians are in the lead. Eddy brings up the rear. His strength is now restored somewhat, but he moves as though sleepwalking.

The group now carries their ragged snowshoes because the snow is firm enough to hold their weight. Most have a cloth of some kind wrapped around their feet.

Foster speaks to the two Indians walking ahead. "Goddammit, you two have no idea where we are. You're lost, and you're too stupid to know it!" Luis and Salvador stop and look at Foster. They both point to a towering ridge. "Oh, Jesus!" says Foster. "How we gonna' make that?"

Later on the ridge, the struggle upward has become a crawl. On all fours they pull themselves toward the crest of the ridge, using everything in their path to help them along. Blood from their feet marks the trail.

Day 17

The group is at the point of complete collapse again. Exhausted, they lie next to a tree that is just beginning to burn.

With their meat supply now gone, each person is forced to use whatever he or she can find to fill the stomach: a piece of a moccasin or a strip of rawhide from a snowshoe.

Wide-eyed, Foster looks at the others. "I say we do what we must." He points to the Indians. "Those heathens are no good to nobody."

"You'd kill them?" asks Mary.

"Why not? We need meat."

Eddy stands and pulls his knife. "Try me, you goddamned coward!"

Foster continues. "Look around. If not them, then it's one 'a us – and soon."

Disgusted, Eddy simply walks away. He goes directly to Luis and Salvador and sits next to them. Luis has uncovered the rags around his feet and is rubbing snow on them. A ghastly sight! The toes on both feet are black and some are even missing.

"Go!" says Eddy.

Unable to find the right words, he points to the others and then makes a stabbing motion into his chest. "You! Go!"

The two Indians nod and place their hands on their chests.

Back with the others minutes later, Eddy picks up the gun and stands before the group. "I'm going."

All five women immediately get to their feet. Amanda is the first to speak. "Going? Where?"

"To find food for us. There must be game out there."

"We'll die without you," says Harriet.

"I'll be back."

"Let me help you," says Mary. "I'm strong. I can help."

"If you want."

The rest of the women crowd around him, physically holding him back. "You'll not come back!" says Amanda.

"I will. You have my word on it."

"At least don't go now," say Sarah. "It's almost dark."

"She's right," agrees Mary. "I'll be ready to go as early as you want."

Eddy offers no response. Rather, he puts down the gun and squats by the fire.

Day 18

At dawn Eddy and Mary are ready to leave. The others, wrapped in their blankets, watch quietly.

"You're leaving us to die," moans Amanda.

""I gave you my word," answers Eddy.

Foster looks around. "Where are the Indians?"

"Gone. Did you expect them to stay and be murdered in their sleep?"

"You're responsible for our death," says Foster.

" Go to hell!"

With that, the two leave the camp as the six watch them go.

It is late afternoon. With Mary at his side, Eddy follows deer tracks as quietly as possible. Suddenly, he stops and whispers, "Mary! Look."

Some eighty yards away a magnificent buck stands next to a small pine tree. Very slowly, Eddy raises the gun to bring the deer into the sights.

Steadying the heavy gun is more than he can manage in his weakened condition. The gun is lowered, and again brought back to its focus on the deer in the distance. Again, his strength fails him. Still whispering, "I can't do it. Bend over." Slowly he takes a step back as Mary drops her head and bends over. She places her hands over her ears. He rests the gun on her back.

104

The deer appears in the gun's sight. A loud shot breaks the silence an instant before the deer leaps into the air.

Later, in front of a fire, the two have their hands and face covered with blood. They work to cut up the carcass as the animal's liver and heart roast on a spit.

Sometime in the new year I think –

More than a day has passed since anyone brought wood. I had no choice but to go myself. I waited until the children were asleep and left. I had to travel far to get even a handful of sticks. Moving through the snow is hard...

Day 19

Eddy and Mary sit eating by the fire. The venison has been cut up and is drying next to the fire.

"I thought they'd be along by now, " says Mary.

"We left a clear enough trail. Fired the gun several times. They can't be lost."

"What should we do?"

"I'll go back and get them. You stay here with the meat. I'll take enough to get them here."

It is now dusk and Mary sits by the fire, looking and listening. She gets up, walks away from the fire, peers into the failing light. Suddenly, Eddy appears, walking directly toward her.

"William! Thank God. What took you so long?"

"I had to go all the way back." He continues to walk toward the fire. She joins him.

"Where are they?"

"Behind me somewhere."

"Are they all right?"

"Fosdick died last night. Jesus, Mary, they were still there cause they were drying his flesh. Had a hard time getting 'em to leave."

"Oh God ... did Sarah ..."

"No, I don't think so. But she was there. Christ, will there ever be an end to this?"

January –

Mrs. Murphy and her children are not at all well. She has shown us a kindness by giving us a share of her hides. I do what I can to help but it does not look good...

Day 22

The group sits before a fire eating their dried meat.

"My meat's all gone," complains Foster. "We got any more?"

"Doesn't last forever," answers Eddy. " It was three days ago we made the kill."

Angry, Foster stands and walks briskly away from the group. He stops a short distance away and turns back toward them. "Eddy, would you help me here?"

"Do what?"

"I need you for just a minute."

Eddy reluctantly rises and walks toward Foster. "What do you want?"

"William, we need more food."

"Go huntin' then."

"Why? What we need is right here."

"What? You're talkin' crazy!"

"Look at Mrs. McCutchen there. She ain't no good to nobody."

"Jesus Christ! She's a wife and a mother."

"All right. Mary Graves. Sarah Fosdick. They ain't married."

Eddy grabs him and throws him to the ground. "You son-of-a-bitch!" He looks around, finds a stick and tosses it at Foster's feet. "Get up and defend yourself, you bastard!"

Foster scrambles to his feet, club in hand. Eddy, raging, pulls his knife and attacks. He is upon Foster before he has a chance to react. In a second Foster is on the ground with Eddy on top of him, the knife at the ready.

The five women, having seen all of this, have moved next to the two combatants. Together, they pull Eddy away as he is about to strike. He stands above Foster. "Keep the goddamn son-of-a-bitch away from me. And all 'a you – watch yourselves. He's crazy!"

Back on the trail several hours later, with the warm sun now above, they have reached open ground. Only an occasional snowdrift serves as a reminder of what has gone before. Groves of live oaks replace the pine trees of the High Sierras. Eddy is in the lead. The Fosters bring up the rear. As Foster trails along, he sees something that has gone unnoticed by the others: footprints across a patch of snow, and bloody ones at that. The Indians!

Foster takes his wife's hand, raises his index finger to his lips, and moves in the direction of bloody trail.

Minutes later Foster discovers the two unfortunates. Next to a small stream, both lie helpless, no more than a dozen feet apart. Foster first goes to Luis. He places the muzzle of his gun next to his head. At the last moment, and with no show of emotion, Luis looks into the eyes of his executioner.

The gunshot, a fairly short distance away, brings everyone to an immediate halt. They look in the direction of the sound, then at one another.

Before anyone can speak, a second shot reverberates through the canyon.

Weeks have passed I know and we grow weaker by the day. All we have left are the hides that I boil and cut into strips and they are about gone. There is not much of value in them but they do help to fill the little ones tummies. I have given up asking the others for help. Even when I beg they seem unmoved by our problems...

Day 23

Eddy and three of the women (Amanda McCutcheon, Sarah Fosdick, and Mary Graves) struggle forward. Somehow they manage to stay on their feet as they place one bloody foot in front of the other.

Suddenly, a group of Indians stand before them. The Indians, shocked and frightened by the horrific appearance of the small party, retreat a few steps when Eddy raises his hand.

Back at the lake a small fire in the hearth in one of the cabins provides the only light. The two small girls, Virginia and Patty Reed, lie on the fire rug in front of it. Except for an occasional muffled groan and the weak whimper of a baby, it is quiet.

One of the girls uses a knife to cut a strip from the scraggly hide that serves as the rug. After that she lays the side with the hair on it next to the coals and carefully manipulates it so that all the hair is singed from the skin.

She scrapes off the blackened portion and places it on a rock where she cuts it into two pieces. One she hands to her companion; the other she puts into her mouth like a piece of taffy.

The flap covering the door is pulled back. Elliott enters. The light now reveals the extent of the oppressive squalor and filth of the enclosed quarters. All the occupants, except for Elizabeth Graves, lie in bed with a blanket pulled up around them. Mrs. Graves sits next to a small cot that holds two infants.

"Hello, Milt," says Elizabeth.

"Mrs. Graves?"

"Come in. Close the door."

"Excuse me, ma'am, but I think you could use a little fresh air."

"Rather have the warmth." Elliott covers most of the opening, leaving only a shaft of light. "What are you doin' here, Milt?"

Come to see if I could get a hide from you. Mrs. Eddy and her children ain't got nothin' to eat."

"Look around you. Does it look like we got anything to spare? I know Mrs. Eddy is barely alive in her cabin. She gives everything she's got to her kids, but look at this poor child." She pulls back a blanket. A shocking sight! Barely alive and breathing fitfully, the child is little more than a belly and a head. "And he's better off than the McCutchen baby." She pulls back his blanket.

Elliott gasps, puts his hand over his mouth and steps back. "Oh my God!" The baby's skin is broken and red everywhere. Lice can be seen crawling all over him. His arms and legs are tied to the bed. "Why are his hands tied?"

"To keep him from scratchin'. Tore his own skin. Won't heal if he keeps scratchin'."

"But the lice!"

"They're everywhere. No way to get rid of 'em all. Besides, I got enough to do just tryin' to feed him. The Keseberg baby is over there in the corner. Died last night. Wanna' see him?"

"Sorry, ma'am. Wish there was something' I could do."

"Doesn't look like you've had much to eat yourself."

"Can't eat nothin' when the little fellers are like this."

We barely move. Writing is difficult. Someone – I don't remember who – brought wood today. It saved our lives. The rest of the time I rub their little bodies to keep them alive. There is nothing to eat...

Day 27

Days pass without the remaining emigrants making any significant progress. Though they have moved away from solid snow, there are still patches along the way. The open grassy meadows and wooded hills are a pleasant site, but now they encounter heavy rains, which stall their progress even more. Grass, nuts - anything they can chew – hardly give them the strength they need, but it does keep them alive. But worst of all, they are lost. Still, they move along as best they can, each step a challenge.

I remember our walks in the warm sunshine Mother. Your smile warms my heart...

Day 32

By this time all but Eddy have given up and lay down to die. The five women and Foster can go no further. With a supreme effort, and perhaps with the image of his wife and family before him, Eddy continues, using every ounce of his waning energy to stumble or crawl ahead.

An angel came to us last night. She was lovely...

Day 33

It is the seventeenth of January, more than a month after they began their trek. Supported by an Indian on each side, a haggard creature half walks and is half dragged along. It is Eddy. His path is marked by blood from his cracked, blistered, and swollen feet; the agony of each torturous step registers on his face.

The door of a cabin at Johnson's Ranch opens with considerable trepidation. A woman carefully looks out. Only when "the thing" in the doorway mutters something like "bread" does she realize that it is a white man. A gasp of horror escapes from her mouth, and she reaches out to provide support for him as she directs him into the cabin.

After being briefly questioned, he is put to bed, too weak to move. A party is immediately sent out to rescue his companions. Miraculously they all survive.

Mother — it is sometime in February I know —

This will be my last effort. The paper is gone and I have decided to burn what I have written to give us at least a moment of warmth and to save you the pain of reading about our sorrowful times. I know my love has reached you somehow as yours continues to reach me. I will save my last piece of paper to use as my final message to my dear husband. If it is God's will he will find it.

Your loving daughter - Eleanor

At the lake, the flickering light from the coals in the hearth illuminates the face of Eleanor Eddy as she lies in bed. Her eyes are open and fixed on the black void in front of her.

A pair of hands gently places a baby, wrapped in a blanket, next to her. Eleanor pulls back the blanket to look at the lifeless face of her baby daughter. Tenderly, she kisses the child. A single tear dots the child's forehead before the blanket slowly envelops the tiny face.

8

RETURN

On the fourth of February fourteen men on horseback and a string of animals set out from Johnson's Ranch in California. At the end of the train is Eddy, still physically weak and barely able to sit on his mount. From their first moments they encounter problems of all kinds. Violent storms rage, pack animals break through the crust of snow and sink to their sides in mud, and gentle flowing creeks are transformed into raging rivers, in which animals are lost in their attempts to cross. Needless to say the progress is quite limited and slow.

At the lake the body of Milt Elliott lies on the floor of the Murphy cabin. Margaret Reed and her daughter, Virginia, sit holding hands on a bed next to the body.

"Can you help me, darling?" asks Margaret. There is no response from Virginia. She merely stares at the body. "Virginia!"

"Yes, Mama?"

"Will you help me?"

"Do what, Mama?"

"We must pull Mr. Elliott's body outside. Bury it in the snow."

"To keep everyone company?"

"Yes, my dear."

"He's so good with children. Mrs. Eddy will be so happy to have him help her with her baby."

"Yes ... I know she will."

By the eighteenth of February a rescue party of seven men use every ounce of their strength to move forward. With large packs on their backs, each step in the deep snow is a challenge.

Looking east, an opening may be seen. The men flounder toward it. A forested valley and the frozen lake in the distance come into view. There is no smoke. No sign of life.

As they approach the cabins they shout to announce their presence and look around for any sign of life. Finally, two figures emerge from under the snow. They are Margaret Reed and Peggy Breen. They both shout as loudly as they can "Here! Here we are! Over here! Oh, thank God!"

The two lead men, Dan Tucker, 48, and John Rhodes, 20, are the first to reach the two women. Both men are struck dumb by the gaunt appearance of the two ladies. The women babble incoherently.

Others, mostly children, now begin to appear. Each is a horrid sight. Their flesh is wasted, their bones protrude. Some laugh, some cry. All seem hysterical.

As the rest of the men from the rescue party arrive they immediately open their packs and begin to distribute the food judiciously.

"Let's get a fire goin', boys," says Tucker. John and I are going on to the next cabin. Keep an eye on the food. Don't give anyone too much."

Several bodies lying in the snow signal the location of the next cabin. The men shout, but this time no one appears. They locate the opening and pull back the flap. The stench of foul air greets them, and they recoil before entering. Inside, there is little movement – only a few heads turn in their direction.

"Jesus! Let's get to work, John."

It is dawn of the next day. Three men, with packs on their backs, make ready to depart. Tucker and Rhodes are joined by Sept Moultry, 42, one of the rescuers. Another member, Aquilla Glover, 45, shakes hands with the three.

"We'll be back as soon as we can," says Tucker. " Get everyone who can make it ready to go. Can't risk getting caught in another storm."

"We'll be ready," answers Glover.

At the forward cabins the three men approach. With them are six members from the Donner tents: Noah James, Mrs. Wolfinger, Leana Donner, Elitha Donner, Solomon Hook, and William Hook. Glover moves out to meet them. "Is this it?"

"We left twelve," answers Tucker. "They'd never make it over. What's your count?"

"Twenty-three. Eighteen of them are children. Seventeen are staying."

"What about Mrs. Eddy?"

"She and her baby are dead. The McCutchen baby as well."

"Oh, Lord! Poor William. Just as well he had to turn back. What about his boy?"

"In terrible shape. He'll hafta' stay. And we better get movin'."

"Sure hope the weather holds."

On the mountain the line has lengthened. The seven men either carry a child or work with several children to move them along. The weaker ones bring up the rear. Little Tommy Reed is unable to continue. His frantic mother does all she can to keep him moving.

"Your boy can't make it, Mrs. Reed," says Glover.

"Yes, he can! We'll see to it that he does."

"He's slowin' us down. We can't carry him all the way."

"What can we do?"

"Take him back. We'll come back for him later."

Now almost hysterical, Mrs. Reed almost screams, "Will you swear to that?"

"Yes, ma'am. I swear."

Patty Reed and Jimmy Reed, Tommy's sister and brother, have been listening to all this.

"I'll go back with him, Mother," says Patty.

"Oh, my darling!"

"Don't worry. We'll make it."

Glover calls to Moultry: "I need you." He joins the stragglers. "Will you help me take these young'uns back to the cabin?"

"You bet," says Moultry.

Glover picks up Patty, and Moultry takes Tommy in his arms.

Patty looks at her mother and smiles. "Mother, if you never see me again, do the best you can."

The two men move away quickly so the children cannot see their mother, on her knees, sobbing uncontrollably.

Hours later the two men carrying the children arrive at the cabin.

Glover calls out, "Hello!"

Breen appears. "What's the problem?"

"These two need to stay here for the time bein'."

"Stay where?"

"Here. With you folks."

"Not here! We have more'n we can take care of now."

"Your cabin is in better condition than the others."

"No, I said!"

"You'd turn these children away?"

"I do what I must to take care of my own."

"Another relief party will be along soon. We'll leave some extra food for their support. Say no, and I'll see to it that your name will be taken in vain by everyone you meet from this day forward."

"All right, but let's see the food."

Back on the mountain the party struggles on. The men, though past their limits of endurance, do all they can to keep the refugees together. *Then* – a rescue party in the distance! Its leader hurries forward. It is James Reed. "Is Mrs. Reed here?"

A short distance away, both Mrs. Reed and Virginia recognize the voice. Mrs. Reed slumps to the snow as Virginia scrambles forward toward her father. Reed picks her up and hugs her close to him. "Your mother? Where is she?" Virginia can do little more than point.

A short while later, Reed stands apart from the group talking with Tucker.

"We did the best we could," says Tucker. "Still, we lost the Keseberg baby, then John Denton died. It's a hard trip."

"That's why we gotta' get goin' right away," answers Reed.

"Does McCutchen know about his baby?" asks Tucker.

"He knows. Still insists on goin'."

As the main rescue party approaches the Breen cabin, Patty Reed is sitting on a corner of the roof. When she sees the men, led by her father, she climbs down and tries to run in their direction. Her weakened condition will not permit this. She flounders in the snow as her father hurries to her side. He lifts her into his arms and hugs her close. All the while she points to the cabin. Mr. Reed responds, "Tommy?" All Patty can manage is a nod before she clasps her arms firmly around his neck. With Patty holding on, Reed hurries to the cabin and enters.

Inside, he quickly finds the boy and drops to his side. "Tommy!" Tommy looks at his father's face, but there is no sign of recognition. When he focuses on his sister, he offers a faint smile.

"It's father, Tommy," says Patty.

Later, Reed and McCutchen approach the Murphy cabin. A few yards from the entrance the mutilated body of Milt Elliott lies in the snow. The two pause to look at it. The head and face are untouched, but most of the flesh has been torn or cut away from the body. One leg is missing. They stand looking at it for several seconds before they enter.

Inside, Charles Stone, 20, one of the three men sent ahead, is at work washing clothes. Next to him, two naked boys, James Eddy and George Foster, lie in bed crying.

"Hello, Charley," says Reed.

"Jesus, Mr. Reed, look at these poor boys. There are more over there."

"Have they been fed?"

"As much as is safe. I couldn't find any clean clothes for them. So I'm washin' the ones they had on."

Reed and McCutchen walk to the bed where the boys lie befouled in their own excrement. Lice are everywhere, and their bodies are covered with the bites of the vermin. Both cry and reach for the two men. The men give them another biscuit, which is quickly gobbled down before they beg for more.

"Jesus Christ!" says McCutchen. "Wasn't there nobody takin' care of these kids?"

A voice from a bed in the corner is heard. It is Lavina Murphy. "Did what I could."

"Mrs. Murphy, were you alone with the boys?" asks Reed.

Stone answers for her. "There's a man in the bed there."

Reed walks to the bed. Several bones lie on the floor next to it. Reed pulls back the blanket.

Keseberg looks up at him, then rolls away. His beard and face are smeared with dried blood, and the bites of the lice are apparent on the portions of his filthy body not covered by clothes.

"How could you let these folks suffer like this?"

"Done what I could," answers Keseberg.

"Goddamn little, from the looks of it," snarls McCutchen.

Reed pulls McCutchen aside. "Mac, we gotta' help Charles get everyone cleaned up. And we'd best take off our clothes before we start or we'll be covered with those Goddamned lice."

Later, outside the cabin, Reed, along with three other men, are ready to depart.

"Do the best you can to get everyone ready to go, Mac," says Reed. "I don't know what things will be like at the Donners, but we'll be back as soon as we can."

Two members of the forward rescue party, Nicholas Clark, 19, and Charles Cady, 20, move out to meet Reed's group as they approach the Donner tents.

Cady is the first to greet them. "Oh, God, Mr. Reed, are we glad to see you!"

"Have you taken care of things?"

"We passed out food, if that's what you mean."

"What are the conditions like?"

"Jesus, Mr. Reed, they're all crazy!" answers Clark.

"Explain yourself, Mr. Clark."

"The first man we seen was carryin' a leg! A leg, you understand? A human leg! When he seen us he threw it into a hole. We looked in and ... there was his head! And a body with the arms 'n the legs cut off."

Cady adds his own description. "Then we seen these children sittin' on a log ... eatin' – Christ almighty – eatin' human innards! There's blood all over 'em. It was awful!"

"They didn't even pay us no mind. It was like we wasn't even there."

"Get hold of yourself, men. How many adults are alive?"

"There's some in both tents," answers Cady. "Don't know who they are. We stayed away from everyone after we passed out the food."

"All right, I want you men to clear some ground so we can move the tents. Then we can clean up everybody and make 'em comfortable for the night."

Two days later, outside a cabin at the lake, Reed and McCutchen discuss the situation.

"Who was alive?" asks McCutchen.

"In Jacob's tent, his wife was still alive – barely. There were four young children and an older boy who'd lost his mind. And Jean Baptiste was living with them."

"Who had they ..."

"Eaten? Jacob Donner, for one. And the other men who had died earlier."

"George Donner?"

"He was alive, but his arm and shoulder are badly infected. Tamsen was in good shape, but she refused to leave him."

"How many did you bring back?"

"Just three. We left nine. Woodworth's relief party can't be more than a few days away, so it seemed best for them to wait for it. Cady and Clark stayed with them."

120

"Then we'll be taking ..."

"Seventeen. Only three are grownups: Breen, his wife, 'n Mrs. Graves. Most of the children will have to be carried, or watched over constantly. And we'll have to leave a good part of our food supply here for those staying."

"Where the hell is Woodworth?"

"His bunch had better get here soon."

Many miles away, Selim Woodworth, a thirty-one year-old overweight armchair-adventurer, sits in his tent having his evening meal. An angry Eddy and Foster abruptly enter.

"What the hell you doin' here?" growls Eddy.

"Gentlemen. Good to see you," replies Woodworth.

"Answer my question! Why aren't you on the mountain? There's people dyin' out there."

"Our guides went with Colonel Reed."

"Guides? Follow the Goddamn trail!"

"We're waiting for a break in the weather."

"Shit!" snarls Foster.

"You got all these men sittin' out there waitin' for a break in the weather?" says Eddy. "You're a Goddamn coward."

"Now listen here –"

"*You* listen! We're leavin' first thing in the mornin'. You'd better get your men off their asses or the governor will hear what a snivelin' son-of-a-bitch you are."

"We were already planning to leave in the morning," explains Woodworth.

"We'll see you at first light!"

121

It is late afternoon, two days later. Each of the four men of the earlier rescue party (Reed, McCutchen, Hiram Miller, 45, and Brit Greenwood, 32) carries a child. They have arrived at a point beyond the pass where the other relief parties had made camp.

"We'll stop here," says Reed.

"Where's the rescue party you promised?" asks Breen.

"I wish I knew," answers Reed. "I sent three men ahead to our cache of goods. They should be back tomorrow. Tonight might be rough."

Two hours later, a fierce wind has risen and it is snowing. The four men have constructed a windbreak out of pine branches against which the snow has drifted. Behind it, and huddled around the fire platform, are the refugees. The children cry and cling to the adults who pray aloud. The four men work furiously to provide enough wood to last through the night ahead.

As the darkness arrives the intensity of the storm increases. Blowing snow limits visibility to a few feet. The men struggle to keep the fire going while the rest huddle close to it for survival.

When the first light of dawn arrives it helps visibility, but the storm rages on unabated. The women do their best to cook the meager supplies.

Breen is outspoken and furious. "We got no food left, goddammit! Where are your men?"

"No one can travel in this weather!" answers Reed.

"You got us –"

"Shut up!" yells McCutchen. "Or take your turn out there cuttin' wood with the rest of the men."

"You know I can't –"

"Hell, we all know what you can't do!"

By nightfall there is still no relief from the storm. It is Reed's watch. The rest are asleep under their snow-covered blankets.

Reed's movements are slow as he places wood on the fire. His beard and eyebrows are caked with ice. His eyes are almost closed to protect them from the driving wind and snow. It becomes almost impossible for him to pick up wood from the snow-covered pile. He slaps his hands together and beats them against his chest. After dropping a few sticks on the fire, he turns to move away. Rather, he slowly slumps to his knees and puts his head down next to them.

It does not take long for the fire to burn down. From under a lump of snow near the dying coals, Mrs. Breen's head appears. When she sees there is no fire she screams.

The first to hear it is McCutchen. He quickly rises and bellows at the other men. In a matter of seconds they go to work to restore it.

One man stumbles over a mound of snow that is Reed. They pick him up and carry him to the huddled bodies. The mass opens up to take him in.

As the day wears on the storm continues. Wrapped in blankets, everyone, including Reed, sits next to the fire. Snow piled against the windbreaks has produced a "bowl" of protection from the terrible wind.

By morning of the next day the intensity of the storm has diminished somewhat. McCutchen wraps the body of young Isaac Donner in a blanket and carries it to the edge of the windbreak where he gently places it on top of the snow.

Reed rubs snow on Mary Donner's feet to combat frostbite. Breen watches him. The men are making preparations to travel.

"You're crazy to even think of stayin' here," says Reed. "You'll all end up like poor Isaac."

"You go on," answers Breen. "We're comfortable here. Without food we ain't got the strength to go no distance at all. We'll wait for Woodworth."

"Goddamn it, man, you can't count on a rescue party!"

123

"Don't waste your breath. We're stayin'."

"Men, you're my witness. The decision is his. The fool won't listen to reason."

Breen's reply is filled with contempt. "Those children you're takin' ain't never gonna' make it."

"We'll carry them!" answers Reed.

Breen finishes his argument by pointing at the huddled mass. "What about the Graves' family? They can't even stand."

"All right. They'll stay with you, then. We'll get someone back to you as soon as we can."

Back at the Donner tent near the lake, there is a call from the outside. Cady rises and pulls back the tent flap. "Charlie! What'r you doin' here?"

"Couldn't take it there no more," answers Stone. "Where's Clark?"

"Out huntin' a bear cub he seen yesterday. Come inside," says Cady.

"No, you come outside."

Cady looks around at the rest who are watching before he steps outside. He closes the flap behind him. The men move away from the tent and talk quietly.

A short while later, the two men enter the tent. Tamsen looks up and welcomes the pair. "Gentlemen, warm yourselves."

Cady is the first to speak. "Mrs. Donner, we're movin' on. You got Baptiste to help."

"What about Mr. Clark?"

"He'll stay with you. You don't need us."

"All right," says Tamsen. "If that's what you've decided."

"If you want, we'll carry out any valuables you have. The Indians'll just rob you," explains Cady.

"Thank you, but I'll take that risk. But, I will pay you to take out my most valuable possessions."

"What's that?"

"My children. You see my three girls through to Sutter's and I'll give you ... three hundred dollars."

The two men look at each other before Cady speaks, "You know we'll be riskin' our lives. Make it five hundred, and we'll do it."

Tamsen hesitates, and then looks at both men before she agrees. "All right, gentlemen. And I'll give you some silver for their support when they get there. Would you wait outside while I get them ready? They need to say goodbye to their father."

An hour later the three girls, Francis, 6, Georgia, 4, and Eliza, 3, dressed warmly in their best clothes are ready to go. Tamsen kisses each and pulls their collars tightly about them.

On the trail, the men carry the two youngest. A look passes between the two men, and without a word they stop, spread out a blanket on the snow and place the three girls on it. After this they move away a short distance to talk. All the while, Frances watches them carefully. Finally, she speaks to her sisters. "Don't worry. I know how to get us back to mother."

The men return and without a word pick up the two girls and resume their journey.

When they arrive at the Murphy cabin at the lake, Cady speaks to Mrs. Murphy. "We're leavin' these girls with you, Mrs. Murphy."

"You can't do that! We ain't got enough for ourselves as it is."

"The relief party'll be along any time," says Stone. "We're goin' on to meet them."

Keseberg's forceful reply is heard. "They cannot stay here! We got nothin'."

"Shut up!" says Cady. "We already saved your life!"

"We'll not take them!"

"The hell you won't!" After what you done, you ain't tellin' nobody what to do!"

"I've done nothin'. We've stayed alive."

"And you're disgusting!"

The two men abruptly turn and leave. The three girls cry softly as they huddle together on the floor.

Meanwhile, Reed's rescue party has halted in its escape attempt. They are most concerned with Mary Donner. Greenwood, examining her closely announces: "This girl ain't gonna' make it. She needs warmth and rest."

"We can't stop so soon," says Reed.

McCutchen reaches a conclusion. "We gotta' take her back, Jim."

"I'll do it," volunteers Greenwood.

"I guess there's no other way," says Reed. "All right, we'll go on slow. Can you pick up our trail?"

"Sure."

At Woodworth's camp in Bear Valley, a group of men are gathered around a fire listening to Eddy who stands before them.

"... lost a day just getting them back here. Mr. Reed has made it clear just how important every minute is. Miller and Thompson have agreed to push on to the lake with Foster and me. We're leavin' right now. Mr. Stone, who just got back from the lake, along with Starks and Oakley, are goin' after the Breens and the Graves. Are there no more men than these with the courage to go back?"

There is a clear absence of volunteers. Most men either look away or stare vacantly into the fire. Eddy continues, "Take no action, you cowards, and you'll have their lives on your conscience forever!"

Outside the Donner tent, Tamsen watches as Clark approaches. "What news, Mr. Clark?"

"Your girls are at the cabin by the lake."

"What about Cady and Stone?"

"Don't know. Gone on, I guess."

"How are my girls?"

"Not good. They're real weak. Too weak to make it back with me."

"Who's with them?"

"Mrs. Murphy. She's sick. Keseberg's there, but he's plum crazy. The Eddy boy died last night 'n he was cuttin' him up when I was there."

"I'll need the loan of some snowshoes, Mr. Clark."

"Mrs. Donner, I –"

"Please, Mr. Clark!"

Seven men from the base camp work their way up an incline with Eddy and Foster in the lead. Directly ahead, Reed's group sits in front of a fire. As soon as they are spotted the rescue party hurries to them.

After leaving them with enough supplies to help them make it back, the rescue party pushes on.

At the Breen/Graves campsite it is late afternoon. The seven men (Eddy, Foster, Stone, Hiram Miller, Howard Oakley, 32, William Thompson, 35, and a giant of a man, John Starks, 25) arrive at the spot where Reed left the refugees.

It is now a huge hole, some twenty-five feet deep, melted into the snow. At the bottom, on the bare ground, the body of Mrs. Graves lies to one side with nearly all the flesh stripped from her arms and legs. Her year-old baby lies next to her mother's remains, crying loudly.

A few feet away lay the bodies of two children, stripped of their flesh in a similar manner to that of Mrs. Graves.

The Breens lie next to a fire, apparently in a stupor. The remaining eight children, also lethargic, seem content to sit quietly.

All the men, except for Eddy and McCutchen, are sickened by the sight; they either turn away or drop to their knees and cover their eyes. Eddy and McCutchen act immediately. They work their way down the crude steps into the hole. Eddy picks up the crying infant and tries to calm it while McCutchen finds a blanket to cover the mutilated bodies.

At dawn of the next day seven men talk near the rim of the "bowl."

"You can't do it," says Eddy.

Starks disagrees. "Said we'd get 'em out, and we will."

"As far as I'm concerned, the Breens can stay where they are," adds Stone. "I'll take the baby."

"I'll take Mary Donner," offers Oakley.

Starks offers his sarcastic response. "Sure, hurry back and get your money. I'll get 'em out even if I have to carry 'em all myself."

Foster speaks weakly, "This is more than –"

"Your job's a lot tougher than ours. Get to those boys of yours. I'll handle this," says Starks.

Eddy pats him on the shoulder. "Thanks, John."

By the twelfth of March four men draw near the Murphy cabin. Mutilated bodies and body parts lie about. They do their best to ignore the ghastly sight by maintaining their focus on the cabin. Eddy calls out, "Hello!"

Tamsen appears almost immediately. "Oh, thank God!"

Hiram Miller rushes forward to hug her. Eddy and Foster, intent on finding their boys, move past them to enter the cabin. Tamsen's lip quivers as she watches them go. She buries her face in Miller's chest.

Eddy is the first to enter. Keseberg is standing in the middle of the room. "Mr. Eddy. I ate your boy!"

Unable to fathom the full meaning of this statement, Eddy merely stands looking at the cadaverous and emaciated figure before him.

"You did what!" screams Foster.

The sound of Foster's voice shocks Eddy back to reality. He grabs Keseberg and throws him against the wall and raises his hand to strike him. The pathetic creature quickly drops to his knees and cowers on the floor next to his bed. "He was dead! Weren't my fault!"

"What about my boy?" demands Foster.

"Dead, too," answers Keseberg.

Eddy moves to where Keseberg crouches in fright and stands towering above him with his fists clenched. Tears stream down his cheeks. Finally, he moves toward the door. Before he goes outside he turns and faces Keseberg.

"You miserable son-of-a-bitch! If you make it to California I'll hunt you down like a dog and kill you!"

Later, outside the cabin, Eddy stands alone, looking at the mountains in the distance with tears running down his cheeks. The sound of the promise he made to his wife months ago in Belleville plays over and over in his mind:

"I know how you feel, darlin'. I promise you I'll always take care of you and the kids. You'll have nothin' to worry about."

After allowing a decent amount of time for Eddy to be alone with his thoughts, Tamsen slowly approaches Eddy. "Sorry about your boy, Mr. Eddy." After he does not respond, she continues, "I have money. If you'll take my girls –"

"I don't want your money. We'll take your girls out. Best get them and yourself ready."

"I'll stay."

"What!"

Foster joins them, and Tamsen continues her explanation. "My place is with my husband."

"Mr. Donner's alive?" asks Eddy.

"Yes, but he won't live long."

"Who's with him?"

"Jacob's boy, Mr. Clark, and Baptiste. If you could wait until I go back to see how he is."

Foster tries to explain. "We don't have the time. We got no extra food. If another storm — "

"He's right, Mrs. Donner," agrees Eddy. "We'll take out your girls and the Murphy boy, but we can't afford a delay."

"You're strong and healthy," says Foster. "Come with us, Mrs. Donner."

"I belong with my husband."

"Sorry we can't wait, Mrs. Donner," says Eddy.

"God bless you for takin' my girls."

Two days later, Tamsen arrives at the Donner compound. She enters the tent and walks directly to her husband who lies in bed. She watches him for several seconds before his eyes open.

"Hello, mother."

"Hello, my dear."

She kisses him and looks at her nephew, Sammy, 4, lying in a bed on the other side of the tent. "How's Sammy?"

"Seems to be all right. Any news?"

"Wonderful news! A rescue party arrived at the lake. Hiram was with them. Mr. Eddy and Mr. Foster were there. They're taking our girls to safety."

"Thank God. Why didn't you go?"

"Rather be with you, my dearest. Where are the men?"

"Gone."

"Gone! Where?"

"Packed up 'n left a couple 'a days ago. Can't really blame 'em."

"Guess you're right. Surprised they stayed as long as they did."

"I want you safe 'n outta here."

"Enough talk for now. Let me look at that arm."

Two days later in an open area near the Donner tent, Tamsen shovels the last bit of snow into the hole that is Sammy's gravesite. "Rest in peace, Sammy. You're with God now." She turns and slowly trudges back to the tent.

Inside, she sits at her husband's bedside where he is crying uncontrollably. "Mother, you must be with your children! Your girls need you. Go!"

"Hush, now. Rest, my dear."

Outside the Murphy cabin three days later, Tamsen calls to anyone inside. "Hello! Anyone there?"

Keseberg, lying in bed by the fire, quickly rises and goes to the door and opens it. Tamsen, soaked to the skin, stands on the other side.

She seems dazed and somewhat hysterical. Keseberg looks even worse than before.

"Mrs. Donner! You're all wet. You must be frozen. Come inside quickly!"

"I fell into a stream. It was so dark."

"Warm yourself by the fire. I'll put on some more wood." He puts more wood on the fire and then gets a blanket to wrap around her as she stands before it.

"My husband died. Today."

"I thought I was the only one alive."

"Then you're alone, too? What about Mrs. Murphy?"

"She died ... oh, a very long time ago. And ... you're alone as well?"

"I am, but not for long. I'm on my way to be with my girls. They need me. If I can just get warm first."

"You're going by yourself? Alone, across the mountain?"

"Soon as my clothes are dry. Others have made it."

"I can give you some of my wife's clothes. They're right here."

"Thank you. That would be very nice."

"Don't you think you should wait until morning? You might fall into the water again."

"Perhaps. You may be right."

"And you need rest. You're welcome to my bed here, by the fire."

"Oh, no thank you. The floor will be fine."

"Please. It's the best spot. I'll wake you as soon as the sun comes up."

"You don't think my girls would mind another night without their mother do you?"

"One more night can't hurt."

Several hours later, in the middle of the night, wrapped in a blanket, Tamsen lies asleep on the bed in front of the coals that remain. The flickering light from the hearth dances across her face. Ever so slowly, a shadow slides across her body and finally blocks the reflected light from below.

A sharp thud, as is made by a heavy object crashing down on a softer object below, shatters the silence.

MEMBERS OF THE DONNER PARTY

The three original families, with teamsters and employees, who left Springfield numbered 32. That included the George Donner Family, consisting of *George*, 62, his wife, *Tamsen*, and their three children, *Frances*, 6, *Georgia*, 4, and *Eliza*, 3. Two other children *Elitha*, 14, and *Leanna*, 12, by George's deceased wife, also accompanied them.

The Jacob Donner Family consisted of *Jacob*, 65, wife *Elizabeth* and their children, *George Jr.*, 8, *Mary*, 7, *Isaac*, 5, *Samuel*, 4, and *Lewis*, 2. Also traveling with them were *Solomon*, 13, and *William*, 11, Elizabeth's children from a former marriage.

Traveling with the Donner brothers were their teamsters: *John Denton*, 28, *Noah James*, 20, *Hiram Miller*, age unknown, and *Samuel Shoemaker*, 25. Also, *Antonio* (last name unknown), 23, who was hired as a cattle herder in Independence.

With the James Reed family was *James*, 45, his wife *Margaret*, 32, and their children, *Virginia*, 12, *Martha*, 8, *James*, 5, and *Thomas*, 3.

James Reed's employees were *Milt Elliott*, 28, *Walter Herrron*, 25, *James Smith*, 25, *Baylis Williams*, 24, and *Eliza Williams*, 25.

Joining the original party at Little Sandy Creek in Wyoming was the Breen Family, consisting of *Patrick*, 40, his wife, *Peggy*, 40, and their children, *John*, 14, *Edward*, 13, *Patrick Jr.*, 11, *Simon*, 9, *Peter*, 7, *James*, 4, and *Isabella*, 1.

Joining the Party in the Wasatch Mountains were *Franklin Graves*, 57, his wife, *Elizabeth*, 47, and their children, *Sarah Graves Fosdick*, 22, and her husband, *Jay Fosdick*, 23, *Mary Ann*, 20, *William*, 18, *Eleanor*, 15, *Lavina*, 13, *Nancy*, 9, *Jonathan*, 7, *Franklin*, 5, and *Elizabeth Jr.*, 1.

John Snyder, 25, was a teamster for the Graves family.

Lewis Keseberg, 32, his wife, *Philippine*, 22, and their children, *Ada*, 3, *Lewis Jr.* 1.

Karl Burger, 30, teamster for Keseberg.

Lavina Murphy, 50, and her family consisting of *John*, 15, *Mary*, 13, *Lemuel*, 12, *William*, 11, *Simon*, 10, *Sarah Murphy Foster*, 23, and her husband, *William Foster*, 28, and their child, *George*, 4. In addition, *Harriet Murphy Pike*, 21, *William Pike*, 25, and their children, *Naomi*, 3, and *Catherine*, 1.

Joining the Donner Party at Fort Bridger were *William McCutchen*, 30, his wife *Amanda*, 24, and their child, *Harriet*, 1. Also a teamster, *Jean-Baptiste Trudeau*, 23.

Patrick Dolan, 40.

Hardkoop (first name unknown), 60.

Joseph Reinhardt, 30.

Augustus Spitzer, 30.

Charles Stanton, 35.

Wolfinger (first name unknown), and his wife, *Doris,* 30.

And, of course, *William,* 28, and *Eleanor Eddy*, 25, his wife, and their two children, *James*, 3, and *Margaret*, 1.

SURVIVORS

Patrick Breen

Peggy Breen

John Breen

Edward Breen

Patrick Breen Jr.

Simon Breen

Peter Breen

James Breen

Isabella Breen

Elitha Donner

Eliza Donner

Frances Donner

George Donner II

Georgia Donner

Leanna Donner

William Eddy

Sarah Graves Fosdick

Sarah Murhy Foster

William Foster

Eleanor Graves

Elizabeth Graves, Jr.

Jonathan Graves

Lavina Graves

Mary Ann Graves

Nancy Graves

William Graves

Walter Herron

Solomon Hook

Noah James

Lewis Keseberg

Philippine Keseberg

Amanda McCutchen

William McCutchen

Mary Murphy

Simon Murphy

William Murphy

Harriet Murphy Pike

Naomi Pike

James Reed

James Reed, Jr.

Margaret Reed

Martha Reed

Thomas Reed

Virginia Reed

Jean-Baptiste Trudeau

Eliza Williams

Doris Wolfinger

THOSE WHO DIED

Karl Burger

John Denton

Patrick Dolan

George Donner

Tamsen Donner

Jacob Donner

Elizabeth Donner

William Hook

Isaac Donner

Lewis Donner

Samuel Donner

Eleanor Eddy

James Eddy

Margaret Eddy

Milford Elliott

Jay Fosdick

George Foster

Elizabeth Graves

Franklin Ward Graves

Franklin Ward Graves, Jr.

Luke Halloran

Ada Keseberg

Lewis Keseberg Jr.

Sarah Keyes

Harriet McCutchen

Lavina Murphy

John Landrum Murphy

Lemuel Murphy

Catherine Pike

William Pike

Joseph Reinhardt

Samuel Shoemaker

John Smith

John Snyder

Augustus Spitzer

Charles Stanton

Baylis Williams

Antoine

Luis

Salvador

ABOUT THE AUTHOR

After a career in Education, during which time he published eight books, Jack Richards is now focused on writing screenplays and novels. He and his wife live in Northern California. They have three children and six grandchildren.

OTHER NOVELS:

Dormant Enhancement I

Dormant Enhancement II

Return (4 Novellas)

CPSIA information can be obtained
at www.ICGtesting.com
Printed in the USA
FSOW02n1006250914
3154FS